SNAKE BOY

by

Leland Robert Johnson

Wichita, Kansas
2006

Illustration and text design by Dana F. Johnson.

Copyright © 2006 by Leland R. Johnson, Jr.

All rights reserved. No part of this book may be
reproduced, stored in a retrieval system, or transmitted in any
form or by any means, electronic, mechanical, photocopying,
recording, or otherwise, without the prior permission
of the author.

ISBN 1-58597-365-3
Library of Congress Control Number: 2005935068

Printed in the United States.

LEATHERS PUBLISHING
4500 College Boulevard
Overland Park, KS 66211
888.888.7696
www.leatherspublishing.com

SECRET WORDS TO THE READER

A man met a woman and married her. . . as men have done for centuries. Growing wise from his wedlock, he glimpsed Truth standing behind the curtain which separates Real from Illusion.

The time came for the man to depart from earthly days when he met his Advocate and asked for another chance at life. He wished to try Truth. The Advocate interceded with the Giver of Life and his wish was granted.

Let the Reader understand that what follows is an account of that which *was* real in an unreal setting, and *what could have been* in reality.

I

Windy March swept winter down a gully in 1932 making way for heated-up April and a too hot May. Warm puffs of air loitered around open doors and windows of Greenhills Public School tempting the more venturesome boys. Attendance dropped as they yielded to the temptation. Word had passed that the springs in Rock Creek were running full and cool. The truancy was officially noted as "illness" on excuse slips over parental signatures that looked suspiciously forged.

The secret swimming was sweeter since girls could not tag behind. Long hair did not dry fast enough and could not be neatly curled, pinned or ribboned to look like what mothers sent off to school in the morning. Besides that, it was a fraternity of "birthday suits" and the membership reveled in their privilege of sanctuary in secret adventure.

A young principal knew the reason for the mysterious absenteeism but let his perception of boy-nature to overrule his dedication to intellectual discipline. Other teachers, not as perceptive, were more dedicated to covering prescribed text assignments, not annoyed so much by irregular attendance as by the wish to be done with what became a hot, sticky school term.

Voices of pupils and teachers blended into a lusty, unanimous "hurrah!" when the flag was lowered, properly folded and the principal shouted a final "dismissed!" Echoes from joyous shouts chased up one valley and back down another, gradually subsiding among the hills as another school year faded into memory.

The noise was barely exhausted when an overstuffed moving van lurched clumsily down rutty and dusty Sixth Street. Its lowered tailgate, held by chains at each side, was loaded with three iron bedsteads and springs, a tricycle with a missing wheel, rusty coaster wagon, washing machine, tubs, wooden benches and an assortment of garden tools together with a crate of pet ducks on top of a box with a pig in it. The entire collection was tightly bound in a web of ropes secured to the sides of the van.

Greenhills was getting a new family to replace the one which left a year before. It was the Baptist preacher, his wife and six children. His arrival brought the town's clergy once more up to its authorized strength of two. For the small community and its large rural area, two men of the cloth seemed adequate to joust with the devil, expose evil and keep goodness flowing in sufficient quantity that passage into the unknown Beyond was assured all souls in the trade territory of Greenhills.

"I heard the Baptists are getting a new preacher," Mrs. Eastman told her family one evening at supper. Her rancher husband was well known as a solid Methodist and as equally well known as the father of six properly mannered, talented daughters.

"Sure hope he doesn't have boys like the last preacher they had," observed Dad Eastman who had heard details of how Rev. Elwood was asked to leave town because his two sons were setting a bad example for other young people.

The older Jonathan Elwood had been in league with Joe, the town moonshiner, whose house was half a mile outside city limits. The police chief did not regard old Joe enough of a problem to call the county sheriff. Not only that, who would dig graves at the cemetery if he turned Joe in?

The younger brother, Harold, had been seen peddling his bicycle along little used Cowpath Road which led to a single house west of town. A cowhand and his childless wife lived in the lone house until he was killed in a rodeo accident. His widow stayed on, finding her economic status little changed unless for the better, when a few unattached cowboys found her attitude toward virtue quite casual and contrary to community standards. The cowboys thought their knowledge of the widow and her ways was proprietary, but in Greenhills and the surrounding counties, there is no such thing as a few people knowing anything—at least about matters that directly concerned the residents. The widow was a problem to the custodians of moral seemliness in Greenhills.

"Well! I don't think Jimmy Smith is any saint," exploded Vivian, eldest of the Eastman six. She jabbed the meat on her plate as though it was Jimmy himself.

"Do you know what that punk told me one time in English Class? He said I had a devil inside me...and I don't!"

"Oh I wouldn't be too sure about that," piped up Lucinda, closest in age to Vivian and the one to challenge her authority as leader of the sisterhood.

"Shut...," broke off Vivian.

"All right, GIRLS!" Mrs. Eastman had acquired the reflexive phrase as a matter of habit when either of the two oldest daughters made a confrontational comment. "That's not a lady-like way to talk."

"Pastor Smith had his problems with Jimmy, no doubt about that," interjected the patriarch of the table full of females, "especially when he started running around with Harold Elwood. Since the Elwoods left, pastor says he's settled down. I doubt that all preacher's kids are bad."

"Does the new Baptist preacher have any girls my age?" asked Jenny, fifth in age, but first in lively spirit.

"According to Mrs. Smith, she thought the Deacon's wife said there were six children."

"Six! Just like us?" Jenny's eyes rounded wide.

"I think she said there were five boys and one girl."

"Is the girl my age?" asked six voices in unison, followed by a froth of bubbly giggling. At the sound of their unrehearsed chorus, Mr. Eastman reared back with an unbridled guffaw which cowhands recognized as readily as the brand on his cattle. Mrs. Eastman smiled then let her silver laughter cascade over the dining table and trickle into the living room.

"The girl is in college, according to Mrs. Smith, and the boys are all younger. The oldest is a senior in high school," she said.

"Boys, ugh!" groaned Jenny.

"Boys, ugh!" echoed second grade Rachael. Mary and Katy, the two middlers, said nothing but you could tell they were thinking a lot.

"I hope he's good-looking," said Vivian vacantly.

"I'll bet he looks like a sick calf," taunted Lucinda.

❦ ❦ ❦

The rusty coaster wagon was first off the truck. Boi took it as a good omen—he would be the first of his brothers to take the town in conquest of the new territory. Picking up the frayed rope that was tied to either side of where the tongue had been, he pulled it out of danger as men began to unload the overburdened tailgate that looked as if everything would tumble to the ground when the web of ropes was untied.

"At least I have all four wheels on my wagon," thought Boi. "Kenny can't keep the little wheel on his trike even with the bent nail and washer on the axle. Kenny is always ruining things."

Then a pleasant thought came to Boi as he looked around at the gathering crew that came to help the preacher unload and, succumbing to their curiosity, to see what kind of furniture he had.

"Plenty of big folks to help move this stuff into the house…I might …" he thought as the yard began accumulating clutter from the regurgitating van. The yard reminded him of an auction he once saw. He wondered how much money their stuff would sell for.

"Who'll give me five dollars for this beautiful chest of drawers with the mirror gone off the top?" the auctioneer shouted.

"Five dollars!" came a reply from somewhere deep in the crowd.

"Fidolla...

Fidolla...

Fidolla...

Fidolla...

Who'll make it six?" chanted the auctioneer as he slapped his hand with a whack on top of the chest.

"Six dollars, for the parson's sake," said a weak feminine voice.

"Sixdolla...

Sixdolla...

Sixdolla...

Sixdolla...

Who'll make it seven?"

A tug on the rope brought Boi back from his imagined auction. He wished his dad would either get rid of the chest or buy a new mirror for it. He was tall enough now that he could see into it if there were one to look at. This possibility made him feel superior to his younger brothers, it would put him in the privileged class with the older ones.

"Take me for a ride." Four-year-old Frankie had climbed into the wagon and rocked forward and backward to urge his "horsey" to "giddyup." Boi looked down at his younger brother and the pleasant thought came to him again. He would pull the wagon along the sidewalks and explore the new town. But should he take his baby brother? If he took Frankie, that meant responsibility and besides, he surely ought to tell his mother and she might not let him go at all. That would ruin the pleasant feeling the plan gave him.

"Ride! Ride!" insisted Frankie.

"Only around the block," promised Boi who decided a short haul surely didn't require parental consent. Slowly he began pulling the wagon along the bumpy brick walk, wheels squeaking loudly at every revolution.

Around the block in Greenhills might mean downtown and back from most of the houses in town, including the Baptist Parsonage. Two changes in direction and as many blocks put Boi at one end of the three blocks of business.

One story brick buildings nudged each other on both sides of the wide, flat, sandy surfaced street. He thought downtown looked like two lines of soldiers on each side of a sandy no-man's land. Each building wore a hat over its front eyes made of corrugated sheet metal. The metal hats were propped up by iron pipes on stone curbs that kept the brick walks from spilling into the street.

The corner building where Boi emerged from the tree lined residential streets was an exception to the brick fronts up Main Street. Its side was covered with vertical boards and battens that seemed to spring out of the weeds at the ground and snuggle under overhanging eaves not far above Boi's head. The high, square topped wooden front hid the shingled, gable roof that extended to the alley. In the middle of the clapboarded face of the building, two large doors hinged inward making an opening wide enough for a car to drive through. Loud hammering sounds rang out from inside and bounced through the doorway, sounding to Boi like a church bell, except what he now heard was a dull clank that didn't have the lasting ring of a bell.

Pulling his wagon to the doorway, Boi peered into the dimness beyond the front opening. As his eyes adjusted to the dark interior, he saw a fire in a bed of coals on a high brick hearth to one side. Nearby, a man unmercifully pounded a piece of glowing, red-hot metal that he held with tongs against an anvil. Boi pulled his wagon into the shaft of afternoon sunshine that settled on the dirt floor. The acrid smell of burning coke bit at his nose but was soon diluted by the dust-covered odor of oil, gasoline and axle grease. Two old men sitting on boxes near the hearth were staring at him.

Boi pretended not to notice the men as he watched the blacksmith pounding fire out of the metal. Abruptly, he stopped hammering and lifted the glowing metal for inspection. Streams of sweat running off his face ended in great drops of brine that vaporized with a hissing staccato on the hot metal. Suddenly he thrust the blazing bar into a wooden tub of water. Boi was entranced by the loud sizzle and hiss that sent a small geyser of steam into the dark rafters of M. Horndecker's Blacksmith Shop.

Boi glanced at the two old men on the boxes and saw they still stared at him. When the water quit bubbling, the blacksmith withdrew the dripping, now dark, chunk of iron. Gripping the tongs with one leather-gloved hand, he shook the glove off the other and reached into his back pocket. Drawing out a huge, red handkerchief, he mopped his face, behind his ears and back of his neck. As he turned his head he caught sight of Boi and his wagonload of Frankie.

"Howdy, son. Sumpin' fer ya?"

"Just watching," Boi mumbled taking a backward step, almost falling on little Frankie. Boi did not think the blacksmith heard him as the iron bar was tossed with a thump on a big wooden bench.

"Yer new hereabouts, aintcha boy?" asked one old man.

"Yeah." Momentarily Boi wondered how the old man knew his name until he remembered that a lot of people had trouble believing his name was really Boi.

"Yew that new preechur's kids?" asked the other old man. Without changing the expression on his face or moving his head, he spat one of the biggest blobs of tobacco juice Boi had ever seen fly through the air. Boi marveled that it could be ejected with such force from such a stationary face. He even thought he heard it hit when it hit the dust, like the hot iron in the tub of water. He wondered how he might evade the question. Some people don't like preachers, he knew.

"Cat gotchur tongue?" came the next without juice.

Boi was thinking. "Nope," he hesitated.

"Ya mean ya ain't the new preacher's kids?"

"Nope. I mean the cat doesn't have my tongue." Boi was careful not to use *ain't*. His dad was a stickler for proper English and had tacked a motto on the wall of his study that said, "Good English is a Matter of Habit," printed in fancy letters with long flourishing lines. Every time Boi looked at the motto he wondered if it would still be true if it had been printed with ordinary letters without long flourishes.

"If'n that cat ain't gotchur tongue, thin who air ya?"

Other activity made itself known from deeper within the gloom where Boi could not see another man working on a car.

"Hey Bill, it's gonna take a two-inch bolt to go through the frame to catch the body bracket." The shouted statement gave Boi a chance to avoid answering the old man's question.

"O.K...got some over here." The blacksmith stepped to a corner where he kept his boxes of hardware. He was not aware that a very small lad had wandered across his path until little Frankie went sprawling onto the dirt floor, narrowly missing the rim of an iron wheel that was leaning against an assortment of farm machinery parts. Missing the rim was fortunate but getting his head caught in the spokes of the large wheel was not.

Frankie let out an earsplitting wail and the men came running. For a few minutes they could not pull him from the wheel. The wide space between spokes at the rim was enough to let his head straight through, but Frankie kept turning sideways and his chin locked him in the spokes as they lifted him closer to the hub.

"Quit yer hollerin' kid. I'll getcha outta here," yelled the blacksmith as he finally saw the problem. Frankie kept up his earsplitting crying as he was put back into the wagon.

"Get this kid outta here!" thundered the blacksmith.

"I'll take him home," apologized Boi who was not heard above Frankie's bellowing.

Boi quickly turned his wagon around and headed for home. The wagon bounced from side-to-side over the rough walk, jolting dirty, bruised, and bleeding Frankie, clutching the sides of the wagon while pouring out air-rending screams. Tears oozed clean from his tightly closed eyes and traced white lines down his dirt-smudged cheeks as they dripped onto his ruined knee pants.

Furniture moving halted as neighbors gathered to find out what had happened. Boi tried to explain to his mother as she lifted Frankie and rushed him inside the house only to come right back out when she realized she didn't have anything with which to clean him or medicine for his bleeding forehead and skinned chin. A neighbor lady surveyed the situation and volunteered first aid and hustled Frankie and their mother to her house.

Boi trailed along. Disconsolate and dejected he sat on the edge of the porch, legs dangling. He wondered how bad the bloody spots were. Maybe Frankie's head had split wide open and his brains would come out! Suddenly, Frankie's screams grew louder. Boi was sure his brains must be leaking out and he felt sick in his stomach.

As abruptly as his screaming increased, Frankie became quiet. Boi panicked. Had his baby brother died? Big tears began to roll down his cheeks. He sure would miss Frankie. He wondered what he would look like in a casket at the church. He saw a dead person in a casket one time. He glanced at the men unloading the van. Should he go over and tell them that Frankie was dead? At least his Father ought to know. How could he say it?

"Dad, I killed Frankie." That would make his Father angry for sure. He would get the razor strop for his terrible deed. Boi could not hold back anymore and jumping up, ran sobbing to the door to tell his mother he did not mean to get Frankie killed.

"Frankie, Frankie! I didn't mean to make it happen to you!" At that moment Frankie appeared inside the screen door looking at Boi. A small bandage covered the scratch over the bump on his forehead and iodine was smeared under his chin, his pink cheeks were cleaned, polished and dry, but big round tears still hung from his wet eyelashes like miniature Christmas tree baubles. He was quiet and held a big apple at his mouth without biting it. So that was what made his yell louder, thought Boi looking at the iodine; then looking at the apple, and that was what turned him off so fast.

"Let's go home, Frankie," said Boi as a burden was lifted off his shoulders. Opening the door, he held out his hand to make sure Frankie did not harbor a grudge. For a long time Frankie simply looked at his brother, then with the speed of a snail, slowly took Boi's hand, still tightly pressing the apple to his mouth without taking a bite. Boi led Frankie home.

Responsibility is a terrible thing, thought Boi, and he wished he could hurry and grow up so he could leave home and not have it anymore. After all, if he didn't have responsibility, he wouldn't have been shamed in front of everyone and he wouldn't have to feel guilty for his feeling of excitement about exploring the town. Now his brothers would possibly explore it before he did. Boi was miserable.

II

A week is a long time to a growing-up person, especially a boy who is curious about things. A whole town can be explored, brick by brick in its bumpy sidewalks, and all its sights and sounds and smells examined at least once; that is, if the town is the size of Greenhills and neatly tucked away in a valley among countless hills that spread in every direction for miles to the distant horizon. The region was famous for the grass-covered slopes and had become known as the Big Pasture where ranchers fattened thousands of cattle each year on the lush strands of bluestem grass.

A week is much longer than a bandage was needed on Frankie's forehead. By the third day, the clean, white dressing had become dirty and the tape no longer stuck to the blue-black bruise. His mother said the cut had healed well enough that if he didn't knock the scab off, Frankie wouldn't need the bandage. Boi was sure glad for scabs. People would never grow up if there were no scabs to plug the bleeding. Kids would just bleed to pieces.

Boi was ready to explore a bigger world than the town.

In one walk to the south end of Main Street, he found Rock Creek running through a concrete culvert that tunneled under the roadway. He wondered where it came from and where it went. The rushing stream sparkled so clearly that its pebbly bed seemed to dance and move in the bright sunshine. Boi was fascinated. For a long time he watched from above, then, coming down from the road, he squatted barefoot on larger stones half in and half out of the shallow stream.

A few yards downstream from the culvert he found a place that widened into a quiet pool. When he stood very still in the ankle deep water, minnow sized fishes would swim around him. Water insects darted on the surface paying no attention to his bare feet. Occasionally he found a crawdad and tried to get it to clamp its big pincers onto a stick. Periwinkles and snails seemed everywhere. The water was teeming with all kinds of life wherever he looked. Where did this life come from and where did it go?

Early one morning while all but his dad slept, he spooned down a bowl of corn flakes soaked in milk. Making sure the front screen door did not slam shut, he left the house and walked to Main Street. Business was asleep along the deserted no-man's-land street, except for Mr. Horndecker who sat smoking his pipe while sitting on a two foot length of sawed tree trunk that propped the in-swinging door to his blacksmith shop. Boi did not know if the blacksmith was still angry with him for what happened to Frankie, nor did he care to find out.

The casual traveler passing through Big Pasture country could easily get the impression that not a single tree grew in the entire region, unless he traveled the county road that led to Greenhills. Taking the county road would lead him to the corner where travelers would likely stop at Smitty's Service Station to be gassed and watered. There in the valley, he would discover a long stand of trees that made for a dense growth or timber that was perpetually watered by springs and Rock Creek as it weaved back and forth from one grassy slope after another.

The traveler would take the county road into town and miss the turn down the dusty road that followed the timber and stood between it and the deep grass that nearly swallowed the barbed wire fence which bounded it. Boi was curious about the timber and Rock Creek so he turned at Smitty's Corner, leaving shoe prints in the deep dust of the little used road.

Butter-yellow meadowlarks with soot-black vees on their throats piped "cheer-i-le-eo" from fence posts before sailing off to disappear in the sea of waving grass. Startled turtledoves fanned the air with their wings making a squeaky whistle as they fluttered into thorny hedge trees. The dense undergrowth kept Boi from entering the woods until a small clearing let him pass a little grove of redbud trees near a towering old cottonwood.

The weeds scratched and tugged at his pant legs as if resenting his intrusion and warning him to keep out. Once inside the timber, his going was easier. Ahead was an old, rotting tree trunk half-covered by a rambling gooseberry bush. At sight of the little green berries, his mouth turned sour as he remembered the gooseberry pie a lady once brought to his mother. Pushing past a scratchy cedar he came to a grassy place where the trees stood back and a big hole in the leafy roof let a bright patch of sky fall to the ground. What he saw in the "outdoor room" astonished him.

Three straight poles had been stuck in the ground and leaned together like a tepee. The grass and leaves had been cleared around the base and the exposed black earth was ringed about by a line of small rocks. At one side of the construction, a large branch of an ancient elm split from the thick trunk, though still attached, swept onto the ground. The opposite side of the room was open to a gentle slope that snuggled Rock Creek along its border.

Boi ran to see his friend running clear and sparkling over its rock scrubbed bed. Exploring up-and-downstream he came to several quiet pools where he tossed in rocks that went "ker-plunk." He found small, flat stones that he had learned to throw and skip them across the water from one pool to another.

Boi returned to the branch and found a comfortable crotch to lie in, almost as good as a hammock, he thought. Looking at the big patch of blue through the tree tops, he saw big, black crows circling around as they rasped a raucous "kaw…kaw… kaw…." At the moment he felt at great peace and closed his eyes to bathe in sound and smell.

Suddenly, the crows became silent and he had the strange feeling that someone or something was nearby. Half opening his eyes, he rolled his head to one side and saw nothing—at first. Then something did move. On the other side of the tepee and in the opening near the stream, Boi saw someone pointing at him as if signaling to somebody else and raising a finger to lips for silence. He sat up and saw three people staring intently at him.

Kids from town, he thought, only they were not dressed like ones he had seen there. Instead of bib overalls they wore cowboy pants and bright plaid shirts. Girls! They were girls, he was sure by their long, ribboned pigtails touching their shoulders. The tallest was about his size; the next about a head shorter, and the small one about half as high as the tallest. The one his size stood in front clenching a long straight stick aimed in his direction. He wondered if it had a sharp-pointed end. It looked like a spear. He had read about spears having poison on them.

The middle-size girl was holding a long stick like a staff. It had a fork at the upper end. The smallest girl peeked from behind the middle one and carried what looked like an overgrown twig. The three stood like statues. Boi wondered if they were breathing. Three pairs of unblinking eyes held him fast to the tree branch. He was reminded of the old men in the blacksmith shop and wondered if everyone around Greenhills just looked at you.

"Hello." Boi tried to sound friendly after what seemed an embarrassingly long, silent time of staring.

"Who are you?" asked the tallest of the three and the smallest came from behind the middle one. Boi thought he heard a menacing tone in her question.

"Boi," in his most unthreatening way.

"We know you are a boy. What's your name?"

Boi recognized his old problem of name. "That is my name. B-O-I, Boi."

"That's a funny name! Where'd you come from?"

He doubted they could do much harm to him and felt a flow of confidence. He would take charge of the situation. Why should he answer their questions?

He'd show them he was not the mouse in their cat-and-mouse game.

"I dropped in from the sky!" nodding his head towards the hole in the leafy ceiling above. That stopped them. He congratulated himself for having been so shrewd until the middle one cut him down from his lofty condescension with, "Oh yeah! I don't believe it. You're not telling the truth. You're lying! You're a bad boy. Go home and have your mother wash out your mouth for lying!"

"Go home, bad boy!" the littlest one took several threatening steps and flourished her twig at Boi.

He walked toward the tepee trying his best to show an air of confidence, then asked, "Did you make this?" It was his turn to ask questions.

"None of your business, and you'd better not touch it either or we'll tell our Dad," said the biggest.

Boi now deduced they must live somewhere close by. He put his hand on one of the poles to show his disdain for their hostility.

"Where do you live?" Boi struggled to regain control of the situation.

"That's none of your business, and if you don't leave right now, we're going to tell our Dad and he's got a gun!"

Boi dropped his hand and stood looking at the three. Silence. He did not know he had just encountered the three Eastman girls. He looked from one to the other. Not only were they dressed alike, but to Boi they looked like they came from the same family. "I'll bet you're sisters."

"None of your business and you'd better go home," the oldest reminded him.

"What kind of gun does he have?" Boi kept grabbing for conversation. He was not on the verge of leaving his greatest discovery of the day.

"He's got two!" said the middle girl.

"Yeah," piped up the little one.

"A rifle and a shotgun. The shotgun is for snakes and the rifle is for coyotes and cattle rustlers."

"You mean he shoots people?" Boi was interested in what their dad did and wanted them to know it.

"Sure," said the middle one.

"Sure," echoed the littlest, then added, "and he'll shoot you, too, if you don't go home, bad boy."

The oldest giggled.

That broke the tension and Boi decided they were not as ferocious as they were trying to sound. He had more time to find out who they were and what they knew about this place and where they lived and a lot of other valuable information he was now curious about. The oldest lowered her spear and planted it upright to wait for his next comment. Boi was wondering what he could ask that would not evoke another "none of your business and you'd better go home" answer.

    He eyed the staff of the oldest. It was not exactly a spear but the upraised end had been whittled to a dull point. Small branches had been trimmed from the stem, which Boi thought must have been a sapling tree since it was so straight, and at least six feet in length. He made an appraisal of the staff and was about to ask a question when a movement in the grass less than two yards from the oldest girl snapped his eyes to the spot.

    "SNAKE!" he shouted and pointed at the same time.

    Three faces instinctively looked in the direction he pointed and three shrill screams shattered the air. The oldest gave a sudden leap and ran straight towards Boi. The other two came rushing behind. Boi was ready to run, too, but when the girls came at him for protection from the common danger, a little courage commanded him to stay where he stood as he struggled to control the fear the sight of the snake raised in him. As he thought about it later, he was sure that if the girls had run back into the woods and left him alone, he most certainly would have fled for home—and not to get his mouth washed out.

Now faced with protecting three other human beings, Boi began to have man feelings and decided he must deal with this threat in a manly way. A manly way was to use his head and not just instinctively scream the way these silly girls were. Boi stood still while the girls crowded behind him. His duty was clear. He must show strength to them while he built up fortitude for himself. This is the role of a man, he thought.

The snake moved, stopped, raised its head and looked in Boi's direction as its tongue made lightning jabs into the air. Boi felt another strong urge to run—maybe he should show the girls the way to the road. No, that would be cowardly and besides, the snake was more that ten steps away which gave him time to figure some way to kill it. He was sure it would not strike from that distance.

"What kind is he?" asked the oldest as the screaming subsided.

"I don't know." Boi's experience with snakes was limited to a small garden snake his older brother once kept in a shoebox, and to a time when a friend had showed admiring boys his bull snake that was big and jumped at you with a hiss and scared the daylights out of you. His brother actually handled his garden snake like it was a pet. "They're cold-blooded and like warm hands," he had told Boi.

"I'll bet he's a rattler. Look at his tail," said the middle girl.

"O-o-o-o, let's hope not," the small one wailed. "They're poison."

"Kill him, kill him, kill him!" shouted the girls in unison.

In spite of panic over what to do next, Boi could not help notice they said "Kill *him*" and not "kill *it*." Why did they think the snake was male? Why did they use the masculine gender in the personal pronoun? Boi remembered this bit of grammar his English teacher had taught last year and recalled how he proudly impressed his family with knowing it. Strange what thoughts come to you as you're faced with danger.

The memory was moot. Boi felt more courage build within him when he remembered that another teacher had said knowledge is power. He couldn't see the connection between his knowing about gender and personal pronouns, and his power to kill a snake. So he applied reason to the situation. Maybe if the snake were an *it*, he could kill it easier than if the snake were a *he*. If the snake were a *she* protecting her young, his battle might be considerably more difficult—he had heard that female animals protecting their young were more aggressive than males and that "the female is more deadly than the male!" He cringed at the thought of fighting a deadly female.

"I think I heard his rattler," said the middle girl.

"I didn't hear anything," Boi found he could talk without betraying his panic.

"Jenny's right. I heard him too!" said the biggest girl.

So Jenny was the middle girl's name, Boi noted as he said, "I need a big stick." He tried to sound matter-of-fact, not at all sure what he would do if he had one.

"Use mine," said all three at once and he immediately found three sticks thrust at him.

"These aren't big enough," he said ignoring their offers as if he killed snakes every day as a matter of course.

"How about the tepee?" breathed the oldest willing now to sacrifice their sacred structure. "Those sticks are bigger."

"Nope. Ought to be a big log that would squash it flat." Boi knew he couldn't lift a log as big as he was thinking but was sure it would take one that size.

"There's one," pointed Jenny to the fallen branch that Boi had been sitting on a few minutes before.

"That's attached to the tree. How could I ever get it

loose? Besides it's too big." Boi did see a dead limb on the branch as big around as his arm. It would be about the right size if he could break it off. After considerable tugging it yielded, and he trailed back to where the trio huddled.

"He moved," shouted the little one as she edged to point at it.

"Rachael! Get back!" commanded the eldest. So the littlest was named Rachael. Boi now had two of their names but this was no time to reflect on it as he began breaking smaller twigs from the limb.

At a safe distance from the snake he flailed the ground several times to practice his aim and stroke—he certainly did not want to miss on the first thrust and have the snake chase him all the way home. He wondered if his weapon was long enough. He had heard that snakes could sometimes jump as far as fifty feet, although he had never seen one do it. In fact, his older brother Wilfred's garden snake couldn't jump at all, but it was tiny compared to this one that got bigger every time he looked at it. This surely must be several times as big as the bull snake his friend had that jumped and hissed and scared everyone.

Boi took several steps toward the snake now moving away from where he had first seen it, as if it was in retreat, he thought. So the snake must be scared too, he muttered to himself. "We're afraid of each other." As he cautiously approached on what he thought was its blind side. The snake raised its head again and looked straight at Boi, its forked tongue darting in and out like needle sharp flames. Fear stabbed Boi as he retreated several steps. The girls screamed.

"Kill him, kill him, kill him!" they shrieked.

He tested his grip on the club and found it had turned to pulp. He wondered why it didn't fall right out of his hand. Somehow he was able to raise it in the air. The length...was it long enough? He asked himself repeatedly if he could hit hard enough and fast enough to make a fatal blow in one stroke. Again, he advanced toward where the snake was still poised with its head above the grass, tongue darting in and out, long serpentine body curved back and forth like a garden hose.

"Kill him, kill him, kill him!" chanted the girls excitedly.

Boi found himself between two impulses: to kill until the snake lay dead and to retreat without felling a blow. He stood suspended in two force fields that have driven man ever since *homo sapiens* became *homo erectus* and set out on the long millennial journey to subdue nature. The three girls hysterically urged him to kill for their safety. He was their shield. It was he who must take the force of whatever danger threatened their safety. They depended upon him for their security.

But his responsibility for the safety of other human beings was challenged by FEAR which urged him to run away. Yet he did not want to expose cowardice, or worse, have to live with his own weakness. It is easier for a man to die in the arms of danger than to live in the cradle of cowardice. Boi was suddenly thrust into becoming a man and he must bear the weight of manhood. He felt the load of responsibility urging his nobler self to stand with courage while his base instinct of fright pulled at his legs to run away.

Why didn't the girls run home? They could run yelling and screaming and probably their father would come hurrying with his shotgun. By that time Boi could be well on his way home. He had faith in his ability to run—at least faster than the snake. Its evil gaze again made his grip on the club feel rubbery. But the girls only stood and screamed at him to kill the snake.

They couldn't leave either, for just as Boi was caught between two force fields, they were part of the same primordial construction of nature. They were the dynamics of the drama that compelled Boi toward his reluctant act. Had they not shown terror, Boi would not have even thought of courage. Had they fled, Boi too, would have run away and never felt the weight of that unique responsibility that's supposed to be a part of manhood. Thus their helplessness became to Boi the ancient instinct to protect and save from harm. He tested two steps closer to danger.

The snake was motionless except for lightning jabs of red tongue as it stared right through Boi's courage and riddled his determination. He gripped his club tighter and felt his sweaty palms telling him to drop the stick and run, they could no longer hold on. But somehow his weapon stayed in his hands. Another step toward danger and he passed the circle of stones under the tepee. Then he was stricken with panic — he had chosen the wrong weapon. Stones! He could throw them at a safe distance and flatten the snake without risk to himself.

He had made a grave error in his choice of weaponry. As ready to admit his mistake as to quit the field of conflict, he would have retreated but at the very moment he considered retreat, he saw the tail rise from the grass and quiver with a death rattle. The sound, like dry, scratchy sandpaper, hypnotized him. He realized he was too late. If he were to back away to pick up stones, the rattler would surely strike him down. He was committed to a deed that had to be done in a particular way and he was now beyond the point of turning back.

The tide runs out only to return. A season goes for awhile but returns ever anew in an annular cycle. But for mortal man, time flows in one direction — never to be known from where it comes or where it goes. This mystery does not make time less real, only more valuable. If its flow could be dammed and held in some strange reservoir to be used at convenience, life would be thrown into chaos. The inexorable march of events would stop, get out of alignment, become scrambled, and living would become a senseless collection of events without meaning. Indeed, could there be events at all? In such a nightmarish existence, one might choose whichever he preferred, but preference itself is a child of unwilling experience. Amid the picking and choosing of events by each person, surrealists would triumph.

Boi had passed the point when he could choose his weaponry and was irrevocably committed to a rendezvous with Fear. The shrieking of the girls stopped and they scarcely breathed as they watched the boy raise the club poised to smash it onto the creature of the grass world. With a darting tongue and rattling tail, the snake gave its own notice of intention to strike down the boy. Poison glands were tightening on their sacs to make the pressure needed to force venom into a gash laid open by needle sharp fangs.

Nature paused while boy and snake confronted each other with the age-old purpose of mutual destruction. In the continuum of time arrives one instant when an event is in some strange manner metamorphosed from thought to realness. The infinitesimal piece of time becomes a fulcrum about which the thought pivots and becomes lever to the deed. It is the burst of an infinitely small increment of eternity born into the finite, by which men reckon their lives. It is a position of the stars, a date on the calendar, a fixed integer on a clock with which men reckon their lives. Thought mutates into decision and resolution becomes the watershed between Before and After.

In one great paroxysm of strength born of fear, Boi brought the branch to earth with a mighty blow and felt it hit the body of his adversary. The "cawing" of circling crows got louder. A bluejay screamed alarm and flew an arrow's path from its perch to the patch of sky above. The girls chorused a yell and Boi jumped back to a safer distance. He was not sure the branch did what he intended. The ground was soft from a deep-piled carpet of matted grass and decaying leaves. The blow had only impressed the snake into this cushion of compost. By fortuitous circumstance, however, the branch Boi fashioned had two sharp spikes from the broken-off limbs and was located such that the longer spike penetrated the soft ground and stuck fast like a driven tent stake. This held his club in place while the smaller spike skewered the snake at mid-body, causing it to move in a frenzy of twists and turns.

But freedom was not the snake's immediate purpose as it responded to the challenge with its own reflex of fear. Again and again it struck at the wood, mouth turned inside out while needle-like fangs attempted to puncture and pollute its tormenter with poison.

Boi watched, mesmerized. The girls shrieked hysterically. As Boi's spent strength returned to his veins, he noticed with alarm the snake wasn't even stunned. To his dismay, his job had only begun. Fear was still in the air and he couldn't become fully a man until the snake was dead.

How to do it? Perhaps he had done enough. Now he could run for home and hope the snake would die from exhaustion. He could say he killed it. The girls again took up the chant, "Kill him! Kill him! Kill him dead!!!"

Boi was again compelled to act, but now it was easier as he knew the scale was tipped in his favor.

Running the few steps where he had thrown the girls' sticks with such disdain, he picked up the dull pointed one.

"Katy! He's going to use your pole!" yelled Jenny to her older sister.

Through the blur of his intense emotional preoccupation in combat, the names came clear to Boi. Katy, Jenny, and Rachael. These were the three girls who had made him act with bravery in the face of danger, a danger that he somehow felt they brought with them. But no time to think about that as he cautiously approached the rattler from its middle that was pinned to the ground.

Boi noticed his tree-branch club move at every thrust by the snake and realized it was not secure. He also noticed the snake's head did not strike with the lightning speed he thought it would. Though fast, he could follow its motion and estimated that he could spear it in one of its recoil positions. He also observed that he must act fast as it would soon free itself from his club.

At a safe distance he paused to judge where he would need to aim his thrust at the right time. In one motion he stepped close and jabbed hard at the snake's head. Missed! He leaped back to appraise the situation. The snake now struck the pole he had jammed into the ground next to it and in doing so, changed its angle of attack to become free of Boi's first weapon.

He needed a forked stick and he ran to Jenny's stick. He

had read how forked sticks were used to pin a snake to the ground by pressing just back of the head. He didn't get the fork very close to the snake's head but did pin it to the ground enough that the head had only a few inches of motion. Holding the stick was not easy for him because of his fear. He felt the living, flexing muscles of the snake as they tensed and contorted.

The forked stick linked writhing serpent and boy. Fear flowed from the hunted to the hunter, at once feeding and destroying the courage in Boi's soul. The long, sinuous vertebrae felt hard against the stick as the snake thrashed from side to side to throw off the hated and feared shackle. In its maddened spasm of contorting muscles, the quivering rattles slapped against Boi's leg and he leaped backward, tripping and tumbling to the ground. The girls screamed louder as their champion seemed to be losing.

Boi was back on his feet as soon as he fell and was terrified to see the forked stick fall over as the snake once more attacked the pointed pole that stuck fast. The rattler was entirely free to pursue the battle on even terms.

Boi made his mistake, he remembered, in not using rocks for his weapon. But the snake made its fatal error in not leaving the scene of conflict. Boi ran to the circle of rocks and grabbed the largest about the size of his fist. He carried two in his left hand while he fingered the third in his right to find the best position for throwing. His marksmanship was not good whether throwing rocks, snowballs or playing catch. He despaired of not being as good at throwing as his brothers, but he felt more secure with rocks in his hands than with sticks. His pulse quickened and he barely breathed as he moved into throwing position.

Taking aim at the snake's upraised head he let fly. Too high. The snake fixed its lidless stare on him again and shook its rattles. Boi felt mushy inside. The second rock flew but was too long. Then the snake struck the pole with open mouth but this time did not draw back. Boi wondered if its fangs were stuck as indeed they had. Quickly he threw his third stone and struck the snake squarely on its back causing it to break inches behind its head.

The furious writhing and thrashing stirred grass and leaves but the snake had lost effective control over its body. In the melee of motion, its fangs came unstuck but its whipping and twisting stayed in one spot. Boi now knew he could finish the job of killing he had been destined to do.

Running to the circle of stones, he scooped as many as he could hold in both hands.

"Get me some more stones!" he shouted. "Get some big ones." Katy led the way running around the far side of the tepee and keeping as great a distance from the snake as she could. Jenny and Rachael followed. Boi began pelting the snake with the pebbles—most missing their target. By the time he finished with the small stones, Katy had brought several larger ones.

"Bring me as big a one as you can," shouted Boi anxiously as he noticed his rock throwing was not having effect.

"Here's a big one." Jenny labored with a large flat piece of limestone big as both hands.

"Yeah, that's the kind I need."

The accumulation of stones around the snake had become a small field. Boi heaved the flat rock. It was large enough to completely cover the head and forepart of the viper. With a dull thud the big rock plate smashed full on the snake's head. Boi watched the twisting and thrashing slowly subside and the rattle shaking less between spasms.

The girls huddled respectfully behind. Boi approached close enough to grab Jenny's forked stick and quickly dodge back. He suspected the snake might only be playing dead to lure him close so when he pushed off the large rock it could strike him dead. He tested the large rock and found when he moved it a little the snake made no response. One big thrust and he flipped the stone away and leaped back. Its head had been crushed, mouth gaped wide and fangs exposed as if for one last gash. Lidless eyes still stared, unseeing now. The reptile lay motionless. Boi poked it. No response.

Placing the stick on its back, he felt nothing to indicate life. With short jabs he felt the hard, grating contact with backbone through scaly skin that wrapped soft, relaxed muscles on either side of the sinuous vertebrae. Surely the snake is dead, he thought. Rachael had been clutching a small fistful of sand and mud from the stream and was coming close to throw them at its head.

"Don't throw any more, Rachael." Boi felt in complete command of everything in *his forest*. Also, by knowing the girls' names and their knowing his, the four joined into a human family.

"Look at those rattles!" exclaimed Jenny.

"You sure smashed his head," said Katy. Boi wished they would quit saying *his* and *him*.

"How do you know it's a *him*, Katy?" demanded Boi as he drew the circle a little closer by knowing their names.

"All snakes are hims," Jenny flatly declared.

"Jenny, you know better than that!" (Now the ring was complete.) "You couldn't have baby snakes unless you had mama as well as daddy snakes."

Boi put the fork under the soft belly and lifted it off the

ground. He had not lifted in the middle and the heavier side slid off giving the appearance of being alive.

"It's still alive!" shouted Boi, not really believing but wanting to show bravery to the girls. They backed away half skeptical. He approached again and forked the lifeless serpent taking care to balance it in the middle. Giving the pole little jerks he could make the relaxed, sinewy muscles appear to be moving. The girls screamed.

"He's still alive!" shouted Katy.

"He's alive. "He's alive," echoed Jenny and Rachael.

"I don't care if it is," pretended Boi with impunity. "I'm going to touch it."

"Don't touch him!" shouted Katy, "He'll bite you."

"He's poisonous and you'll die," warned Jenny.

Boi needed one last proof the snake was really dead. The girls' positive opinions had caused him to doubt his own judgment. He knew that ultimate victory could only come when he could grab the vanquished enemy in his fist and not be afraid, since Fear was his real antagonist — Fear that lay in him as the residue of human instinct, added incrementally in each generation as long as mankind had roamed the earth as hunter and hunted.

Being committed to touch the repulsive creature, he decided to do it with the snake on the ground. Lowering it, he half expected to see it slither away into its own world of leaves and grass. It lay motionless, putting the fork astride its neck, he leaned over, standing ready to leap away if necessary, and touched the back. He could feel the hard lumps of vertebrae under the cold, loose skin of slippery smooth scales. The creature gave no response to his touch and he gained courage.

Putting his hand around its neck behind the forked stick, he slowly lifted it into the air, carefully watching for any sign of life and he could drop it instantly. He had to lift it above his head to get the rattle to swing free of the grass. Blood and venom oozed from the mangled mouth. The girls' screaming became subdued to expressions of awe. Boi took this as a sign of admiration for his daring and fearlessness.

"That's a big one!" Katy emphasized *big* and at that moment Boi felt tall, even taller than his older brothers. Now he would have to stoop to see into the mirror of their chest of drawers, if it had a mirror.

"I don't think he's as big as the one Dad brought in from South Hill last summer," Jenny said and Boi came back to his normal size. He realized with disappointment this was not their first encounter with a rattler. Boi lowered it and looked at its smashed head, still holding it at a cautious distance. The girls stepped closer.

Surely the Creator knows what makes a boy think the thoughts that move along in the long dark tunnels and crevices of a twelve-year-old mind. Is it a sense of power over his female counterparts that make him tease them, hoping to let them know who is master? Perhaps he merely responded to girls' taunting that dared him to torment them. Whatever the motive, Boi thought about how they ordered him off this place which, at first, was a pleasant outdoor room but had become a battleground where boy-man and beast engaged in mortal combat. Victory was a man stirring within a boy. Now, surely, the balance of justice gave Boi the prerogative of belligerence. With a sudden hiss and jabbing motion of the snake's head, that in death, was an evil, leering, final triumph of wrong over right, Boi turned on the trio.

The instinctive wild screams were more than Boi had reckoned. Their reaction even startled himself when little Rachael began crying in between screams and all three fled through the clearing. Their screams and shrieks began to lose their way among trees and underbrush as the girls continued running terrified toward their home, Boi assumed, leaving him alone with his snake.

Katy and Jenny deserved the scare, but he felt bad

about causing Rachael to cry. He really didn't mean to go that far – indeed he had not counted on the effect it would have on her. Maybe he shouldn't have done it. For one thing, if they hadn't brought him stones and sticks he couldn't have killed the rattler; which he now trailed in the road as he made his way back to town as his trophy. He found he could wiggle its rattlers in the thick dust and make a trail that looked like a live snake had been there. He made the track weave in and out of his shoe prints to look like the snake had chased him. He thought about what it would have been like if the snake had actually been after him.

He walked past the blacksmith's shop hoping now to be seen. The old man with the unusual spit-range ability was sitting on the tree trunk by the door.

"Where'd ja git th' snake?"

"Out east," said Boi pointing the snake in the general direction.

"Rattler," muttered the old man, then raising his voice to the dark inside, "Bill, you still lookin' fer rattlers?"

Bill came out and eyed the prize. "Give ya ten cents fer 'im."

Boi was astounded that the snake had monetary value. It had not occurred to him that it was worth money to fight a menace and win. He was not sure he wanted to part with his prize so soon, especially since he planned to amaze his brothers with it.

"I'll sell it to you, but I want to take it home first and show my brothers."

"Don't show it to yer ma. She mightn't let you outta th' house fer a week." The blacksmith laughed at his jest, but Boi was not amused. He was thinking of the possibility of being restricted at home – the idea had not occurred to him and it troubled him to think that confinement might happen. He walked home making a mental calculation that, at ten cents each, he would have to kill thirty-one and a half rattlers to make enough to buy the pocket watch he wanted. Maybe the half rattler would be a baby.

His brothers were impressed as were the rapidly informed neighborhood youngsters. Boi proudly recounted his experience for each newcomer who came to see and listen to the rattles and to his account of his bravado. Wilfred, his next older brother, confided to him that he had better leave those snakes alone and not try to kill them. If he were bitten that would be the end of him.

"But I can get ten cents for every one I bring in," countered Boi. "The blacksmith is going to pay me for this one."

"Oh well, I'll bet you can get more than a dime at the courthouse in the county seat. I heard there is a bounty on rattlers 'cause they sometimes bite cattle and kill them."

Boi went to bed that night feeling triumphant. He had killed a dreaded reptile and made girls run. A feeling of power overcame him. Of course he did have some help but he was sure he could have killed it alone. Most of all, he had dethroned Fear. He did feel sorry that he made Rachael cry, though. That was considerably beneath the gallantry of a person with his valor. And Jenny and Katy really did help him. He hoped he would see them again sometime and tell them he was sorry to have played such a mean trick on them, even if he did feel good about it.

He wondered if he had a devil inside. His father once said the devil felt good when anyone did something bad. With his snake safely packed in a box under his bed, Boi dreamed about snakes all night and it almost made him wish he had never seen one, except for the good feeling when he thought about how he could kill them and protect scaredy-cat girls from them. By morning the smell almost caused him to lose his trophy when his mother came looking for the source of the terrible odor.

※ ※ ※

Mrs. Eastman looked out the window over her kitchen

sink. The back yard lay under the canopy of a high old cottonwood tree through which filtered soft summer sunlight. A tire hung at the end of a rope tied to a branch as high as the two story house. Near the swing, yet out of reach of its arc that came within a foot of reaching the ground, a sandbox was enclosed within a square of four 2 x 8's nailed at the corners. A homemade teeter-totter next to the sandbox completed the playground where the younger girls spent carefree summer hours when not busy with chores of gathering eggs, helping with house cleaning or feeding the gathering chickens. The older girls helped with milking and other larger jobs about the ranch.

Past the chicken yard and beyond the vegetable garden laid out with a plot for each girl, Mrs. Eastman looked toward the trees that hid Rock Creek as the watercourse leisurely wandered along the valley, ever avoiding the smooth grassy slopes and round hills that were the fame and fortune of that country. She made a perpetual prayer of thanksgiving to her husband's father for settling on a place that was so blessed with trees and water. If it were not for the springs further back in the hills that ran in dry weather or wet, there would be only dry gullies carved from meager top soil.

Deep from within the timber the girls' screams and

shrieks faintly drifted over the distance and through her open window, distinct enough to alert her. Her practiced ear could distinguish the message each of the six sent by way of their shrill voices. Their vocal sounds were modulated for each circumstances and she knew each of their meanings. Injury and hurt were ragged sorts of noise interspersed with crying and wet tears—not to be confused with feigned injury which was a sort of hollow, mechanical, dry-tear noise that could be abruptly turned on and off according to the pretender's estimate of effect. Screams of fear were easiest to identify and this was what Mrs. Eastman heard coming out of the timber. She turned her head to better hear whether injury might be the cause of commotion and if so, which girl was the probable victim, but all three were shrieking at once.

Grabbing a towel, she called to Mary, kept home to take her turn at cleaning the upstairs.

"Something's happened to the girls. We'd better go see!"

Experience on the ranch taught that anything can happen to children. Seldom had the parents investigated a disturbance without finding a real cause for concern and need for adult intervention. Mrs. Eastman quickly crossed to the open door, out the screened porch and down the walk that led to the fenced chicken lot. Past the hen house and across the middle path that bisected the garden, she hurried with half-walk, half-run, apron flapping on her skirt that could not keep up with her flying steps. Mary sprinted to catch up.

As Mrs. Eastman reached the edge of the garden and started on the path to the timber, Katy, Jenny and Rachael came trailing breathlessly out from the trees. Jenny was first and at sight of her approaching mother, ribbons on her pigtails flew on and off her shoulders like butterflies. Close behind came Katy leading Rachael whose screams had dissolved into hysterical sobbing and a torrent of tears.

"There's a bad boy in the woods!" shouted Jenny as she ran out of breath to the shelter of open arms. "A bad, bad, bad, terrible, evil boy!" Further words were drowned, in the sobbing and crying as all three were pulled to their mother's arms.

"What happened?" Mary came running and asked in out-of-breath excitement. "What happened? Who got hurt?"

"There's a terrible evil boy in the woods!" Jenny cried over her mother's arm and clung more desperately.

After the crying subsided, Mrs. Eastman learned with relief that none of them had broken bones or bleeding, she listened intently as pieces of the story came tumbling out from each. Like a hen with wings spread to shield her chicks, Mrs. Eastman held her arms around the three small adventuresses and walked them back to the house. Mary hopped backwards in front of them to hear the tale of danger her sisters related and was envious that she could not have been with them instead of getting stuck with the dirty old up-stairs. They neared the house and Jenny ran toward the barn.

"I'm going to tell Dad," she called over her shoulder to her mother as she broke away from the others.

"Me too," said Rachael ready to drench her cheeks with more sobbing as she desperately ran to catch her fleeing sister.

That noon at dinner and again that evening at supper the episode was grimly retold and assessed by the family.

"So the boy said he came from the sky?" Dad Eastman queried.

"Yes, but I don't believe him," said Jenny. "I know he was lying and that proves he's evil."

"How do you know the snake was still alive when he picked it up?"

"I could see it staring right at us and something was drooling from its mouth. Then he pushed it at us to make it bite us," explained Katy.

"Besides that, we could hear its rattlers," added Jenny.

"Yeah, I heard them too," said Rachael.

"Another thing," remembered Katy, "he knew all our

names and called us by them and we didn't tell him what they were. Isn't that right, Jenny? Isn't that so, Rachael?"

"Yes, and we have never seen him before. How would he know our names? I'm sure he's evil," said Jenny.

"Yeah," echoed Rachael. "How'd he know our names?"

"How big a boy did you say he was?" Dad Eastman wanted to check their estimate of height again to see if it had increased with each retelling.

"He was about the same size as Katy, like we told you before. And when he held the snake high over his head, the rattles just touched the ground," answered Jenny.

"I don't believe it was alive," countered Lucinda who found that skepticism always kept a table conversation energized. Besides, she wasn't convinced they really saw a boy but had only been frightened by the snake.

"I'll bet he came from town." Vivian hoped maybe he was one of the new preacher's boys. "You're sure you've never seen him before? He may be one of the boys in the new preacher's family."

"Oh no, he couldn't be that," said Katy, "'cause he said his name was Boi, B-O-I. Did you ever hear a *real* person with a name like that?"

"It is unusual, but there are a lot of funny names in the world," observed Mrs. Eastman.

"Yeah, to go with a lot of funny people!" commented Jenny and laughter dismissed the apprehension that lingered around the table.

"Do you suppose…?" Dad Eastman looked at his wife but did not finish until late that night in the privacy of their bedroom when the house was dark and quiet. "I didn't want to say anything in front of the girls about the boy they found in the timber," the rancher said, "but do you suppose he was one of the preacher's kids and they belong to a snake cult?"

"I never thought of that," replied his wife thoughtfully.

"It's hard to believe the Baptists would get a preacher like that, but after the Elwoods, you don't know what to expect. If it really was a rattler, Bill will want to skin it and nail it to the door with the other skins in his blacksmith shop."

"As I remember, that article I read about a snake cult in Kentucky said the people were Baptists."

"Of course there are more kinds of Baptists than states in the union," continued the rancher.

"Katy and Jenny insisted they have never seen the boy before. But how would he know their names? I suppose he could be one of the preacher's boys."

"Maybe so. What was he doing in the timber?"

"Probably just exploring the countryside."

"I suppose so. Those boys had better find out where they're welcome and not just go roaming around wherever the notion strikes them. If I catch anyone scaring my girls, I'll fill his pants with buckshot."

"I'll call Mrs. Smith and see if she can find out anything about the family. If they're really cultists we'll sure have to keep an eye on them. With rattlers around here they'll get themselves killed—maybe someone else along with them!"

That seemed to close the subject until the rancher said, "Funny thing, there's that preacher with five boys and here we are with six girls. I sure could've used some boys in the family and not had to hire so many cowpokes. Looks to me like the preacher would've been better off with girls than boys."

"Oh, Chester! I know you always hoped for some boys, but surely you wouldn't want to give up any of our girls!"

"Of course not, now that they're here. But suppose we'd had three boys along with three girls, I'd settle for that."

"Now just which three would you trade for boys?"

"Lucy would have made a good boy. Katy and Jenny will be good at wrangling, too, I'll betcha."

"Don't try making cowboys out of the girls. Just help me keep them feminine and they'll each bring you a man when they get married," countered Mrs. Eastman.

"Lot of good that'll do me. Ever notice how many young couples stay on the range once they get married? They all head for the bright lights of the cities. Besides, look at your family. Only three out of five girls married and you're the only one with a family of any size. Nope, I'm not waiting for any of our daughters to bring home a man. After Jenny and Rachael came, I decided that this old dad's going to have to hire his cowboys. Some guys have all the breaks. Take Crawford, for example, both his boys are going after ranching like they were born in the saddle."

Mrs. Eastman absorbed an inner feeling of disappointment that she had not pleased her husband with sons, though well aware she could have done nothing about it. It did seem unfair that she had all the help needed around the house — even if reluctant much of the time — while her husband had to hire ranch hands. They tried to use the girls where they could. Lucy was a tomboy when it came to riding the range, but they always felt guilty about exposing them to the hazards a man ought to face.

Heavy breathing by her side said sleep had overtaken the rancher and she knew a light kiss on his prickly whiskers would not disturb his dreams of strong young sons. A tear fell with the kiss and dissolved the Eastman household into a quiet world of night with an occasional thumping from horses in the barn or bawling of a cow dimly heard from a distant hill. In the cool relief of steady night breezes, crickets rasped their wings in a syncopated, squeaky song and frogs around Rock Creek romanced each other under a waxing moon.

III

Boi watched tents spring out of the school's football field the way toadstools magically appear after an overnight rain. The field was the only spot with enough flat area in the vicinity of Greenhills to stake out tents and still leave room for rides and money-spending crowds at the annual picnic fair.

The site had another advantage. It was next to the school gymnasium which was exactly the right size for all the portable wooden tables hauled in from the town's two churches. For one day of annual glory, the gym became a regional Smithsonian for every blue ribbon skill within a twenty-mile radius of Greenhills. Homemakers' reputations rose and fell on their abilities at canning, cake-baking, quilting, crocheting, as well as hand-decorated china, flower arrangements, tatted doilies, needlepoint and dress-making. There was no beauty contest at the fair—not for lack of qualified contestants, but for the order of priorities in the small community's protocol of important things.

The early-day town planner who decided where streets would run had wisely decided to put the school and its football field across the sandy road from the city park. The park's open bandstand poured thick, heavy oom-pahs of tuba, trumpet and trombone into the sultry summer Saturday night air to flow over the town and into open windows where tied-back curtains welcomed every puff of wind that wandered down from the hills and gently snuggled into the valleys around the town of Greenhills.

A few picnic tables were scattered around the park. Families brought picnic baskets to the grove of elderly elm and patriarchal cottonwood trees that spread their lofty limbs over grassy spots now browning from the late summer drought. The school, its grounds, and the park were close enough to a Garden of Eden for the locals that they were the most appropriate setting for Greenhills' anticipated and traditional "End-O-Summer" picnic fair.

Men frantically unloaded canvass, ropes, poles and stakes as if their very lives hung by how much they moved out of the trucks and along each sideline of the football field. By noon, two rows of tents faced each other across the playing field. A canvass city was completed by the raising of a towering Ferris wheel at the fifty-yard line in company with a carousel on one side and a tall, six-sided tower on the other. Swings hung from spider arms extended from a tower that spun riders around into a horizontal orbit.

Boi had been watching from a high slope in the morning sunshine as the man-ants scampered about putting the tent city together. As he watched, confusion and apparent aimlessness gave way to order. He soon realized a plan had been followed and he was fascinated by the rides taking shape in the center of the field like a giant erector set. He decided to have a closer look at how they went together.

Coming down from the hillside, he found a place where he thought he could avoid a "Beat it, Kid!" from the carnival people. He was unaware of a pair of eyes that followed him as he approached the Ferris wheel.

"Wanna make some money, son?" Boi jumped. He hadn't notice a narrow shadow slide over him before he heard the booming voice.

"Yeah, guess so," not sure until he knew just how he would earn it. Work is noble and earning money is good as long as it didn't involve cheating or taking advantage of someone — that was what his parents had said.

"Over this way," said the narrow shadowed man and Boi trailed behind through the work that only moments before looked off limits to him. Now he was one of the man-ants and privileged to walk among them.

"See that tank over there?" The man pointed to a stock tank like ones Boi had seen in pastures under windmills to collect water for cattle and horses. "Now see that water hydrant over there?" The man swept his arm through a forty-five degree azimuth. "If you'll take these two buckets and carry some water to the tank, I'll give you fifty cents."

"Sure," said Boi. The image of a heavy half-dollar blocked perception of the number of trips he would have to make to fill the tank.

At this moment of opportunity, he thought it important to not jeopardize his newfound road to riches by asking how full the man wanted the tank — his employer might think he was lazy and that he questioned the arrangement. Boi turned the handle of the hydrant and the water gushed into one then the other bucket. He thought about how many trips he'd need to make. It ought not take a terribly long time with both buckets. The tank was a smaller version of the one he saw in pastures.

His first haulage was discouraging. The tank was out of level and the high side didn't even get wet for several trips. Another four times and Boi noticed the entire bottom was wet — to a thin depth on the deep side and barely wet on the up side. Greenhills fire siren wailed its daily noon alert as Boi continued the cycle:

gush and fill,
tote and dump,
return to start all over...

gush and fill,
tote and dump,
return and start all over...

"Looks like ya found a good boy, Jojo," observed Popee, the popcorn man. Popee's nickname had stuck among the carnival folks who held him in respect. He made as much money from popcorn as anyone did, even those who hawked the most beguiling attractions and rides. Their overhead seemed as large as the Federal Debt compared to the popcorn man's little kerosene operated machine.

"Yeah, looks like I may have to pay 'im what I told 'im," complained Jojo lighting a cigar in the shade of the huge yellow and white-stripped umbrella that sheltered Popee's machine.

"Whatchya givin' this one?" Popee knew Jojo's business as well as Jojo, but their verbal nod to each other was a kind of ritual at every place they set up.

"Th' same. Ya know, 'sfunny how kids in these small towns all jump at the bait, but you git a town of mor'n a few thousand an ya can't git a kid to even rassle up a hose fer ya." The two looked at Boi now stopping halfway to the tank on each trip to rest his arms that felt like they had turned to wood.

"Jojo, I think you abuse th' boys."

"Now jes' a minute, Popee. I give them kids a fair deal. They know what the job is 'for they start."

"Yeah, but they don't know how you payoff and keep them quiet at the same time."

"What's wrong with my payoff?" bristled the grounds manager.

"Ya know them kids take the job thinkin' they're gonna git fifty-cents. Soon's they play out and say they can't haul anymore, even though it's all the water you wanted to begin with, big hearted Jojo, citizen's friend, says 'well son, ya only finished the job halfway so I'll pay ya fer wot ya done. Here's a quarter.'

Now I'm not sayin' you're illegal, maybe not even disethical, but...well, take that time at Cedar Falls. I wanted that kid t'run my popcorn machine but ya got 'im mad and he didn't come back."

"Lissen, Popee, jes' don't tell me how t'make a deal, see! Ya keep poppin' yer corn and let me manage the midway—and don't fergit yer ground fee!"

"Whaddya mean? Have I ever welched on m'fee?" growled the popcorn man. "Ya know I'm the best payin' concession ya' got. Everbuddy eats corn."

"I ain't complainin' 'bout how ya pay, but I resent yer implicatins 'bout my deals. Jes stay outta my business."

"O.K. O.K. I was jus' makin' an observation. Ya don't need ta be so touchy 'bout it…"

gush and fill,
tote and dump,
return to start all over…

gush and fill,
tote and dump,
return to start all over…

Boi was beginning to wonder if his weariness was worth the heavy coin he could almost feel in his pocket. On many trips he thought about how the man could have set his tank closer to the spigot and run a pipe from it to the tank — like ones he had seen in the pastures.

The shallow side now drowned his index finger. Carrying the empty buckets back to the spigot was the best part of the cycle that partly offset carrying heavy water that steadily got heavier and made the veins on his skinny, sweaty arms stand out like long strings of spaghetti.

The sun had swung to mid-afternoon. Boi wondered if he were missed at home. He was sweat-soaked. Big drops ran down his face, coalescing with little drops to make salty streams that ended in a small shower with each bob of his head. He wondered if he should try to keep from letting his sweat drop in the water. The man didn't tell him what the tank of water was for. He saw bits of grass blow into it so he decided a few drops of sweat wouldn't hurt it. Boi was glad he could sweat since the breezes then kept him cool under the hot August sun.

"O.K. son, that looks like enough. Here's yer fifty-cents." Boi dropped the buckets that practically fell from his hands with fingers that throbbed from the wire handles on the heavy buckets trying to pull his arms right out of their sockets. He wiped his face on his rolled up shirt sleeve like a cat trying to wash behind its ears. "See that feller over there under the big umbrella?" Boi looked in the direction pointed out by Jojo's long cigar. "Tell him Jojo sent ya."

The half dollar felt heavy and alive in Boi's fatigue-swollen hand as he slid it in the side pocket of his over-alls, then taking it out, he decided it would be safer in the watch pocket on the front of the bib. The watch pocket had a vertical slit just big enough for a watch to slide through, so neither watches nor money would fall out even if he stood on his head.

"Jojo sent me," announced Boi to a pair of legs that protruded from the back of the popcorn machine. The shade of the umbrella felt good. A lazy, late afternoon breeze touched Boi's wet face and arms and cooled him with the strange exhilaration that comes when water and air merge to create an invisible vapor around wet, hot skin.

The upper part of the machine had glass on three sides, all covered inside with white swirls of cleaning powder. Boi was not sure the part of the body inside the machine heard what he addressed to the legs outside. He started to repeat himself when he noticed a small clear spot on the glass side next to where he stood.

An eye peered through at him. The spot became larger until it filled with a round, pink face with two black beads for eyes that were in the exact centers of a pair of black, horned rimmed circles. The spot expanded as Popee rubbed enlarging circles on the glass.

"Ever make popcorn before?" boomed a voice deep inside the glass box.

"No sir," though he thought of the many times someone at home made a skillet full.

"Wanna learn?"

"Sure." Boi was positive about this harmless occupation. He was certain his Dad would not object to popcorn-making. "Mind if I go home for a little while? I better tell my folks where I'm working – haven't been home all day."

"Eat something and be back at seven." Popee did not want a tired and hungry lad working for him.

Elated beyond his tiredness, Boi turned the corner on Sixth Street. Kenny and Frankie were playing on the gunnysack swing that Edwin and Wilfred had hung from a branch of the high arching elm tree.

"Did you get paid for carrying water?" Kenny yelled when he saw Boi coming.

"Of course. You don't think I'd do all that for nothing do you? How'd you know what I've been doing?"

"Edwin and Wilfred saw you. They told Mama."

At least they didn't know how much he was paid and they didn't know about his popcorn job. He had two surprises left for them.

"Where have you been all day?" Boi's mother asked.

"I thought Edwin and Wilfred told you," countered Boi as he wondered if his mother was testing him for the truth.

"They said they saw you at the carnival grounds with the carnival people. Is that the only place you've been?"

"Yes, well, I did go up on top of Heathrow Hill at first and watched for awhile. When I came down to see the men put the Ferris wheel together, a man asked me if I wanted to earn fifty cents." Boi drew the half dollar from his watch pocket. "Look! Not only that, Mama…" Boi eagerly broke the news about his popcorn-making job as he trailed his mother around the kitchen while she fixed supper. "You think Dad will care?"

"I don't know. We'll have to ask him when he comes in. There's nothing wrong with making popcorn. Looks like you'd better let me iron you a clean shirt. Have you got some clean overalls?"

Boi's mother was late with supper, as usual, but after a few fast bites of wiener and sauerkraut and sweetened rice with milk "getting chummy in his tummy" (he could always make Frankie laugh with that), he left the house with a slab of bread and butter sprinkled with sugar in his hands and an admonition from his father in his ears about girlie shows. He really hadn't thought about the carnival having girlie shows and he wondered what they did that would draw such a stern warning from his dad.

Boi arrived on the grounds amazed to find lights blazing around the tents and on the rides before it was yet dark. Like moths, people were already gravitating to the gaudy attractions that wouldn't wait for sunset. Popee had a big drift of popped corn in the glass bin.

"Thought you weren't coming back," Popee reproached Boi and told him if he was going to sell popcorn he would have to be around when people were there.

"Yes, sir," Boi responded.

"Now see that sack," asked Popee pointing to a large bag of unpopped corn. "There's the corn. Take this tin cup..." Popee showed Boi exactly how much corn to put in the popper, how much butter went into the butter trough and salt went into the shaker.

"If you fill these right, your corn will come out perfect every time. When the 'snow' spills over the top of the popper, turn this crank and it'll empty the popper. Butter and salt will hit it exactly right." Boi learned that "snow" was carnival jargon for corn that had been exploded into beautiful, fluffy white shapes. A favorite game at home was to see who could find the most unusual animals that popped out of the little grain prisons. He sure didn't have time to look for animals in the huge drifts coming out of this popper, though.

"Here's the way to fill the boxes," went on Popee as he showed Boi how to open the collapsed boxes, fold the bottom flaps shut by fitting tabs into slots, fill with one scoop of 'snow,' and snap the top flaps shut.

"Box up all this snow and while you keep boxin', make that popper work all the time. You have to keep workin' fast, see kid? Once people get hungry and start buyin' snow, you'll sell lots of it."

Popee was right, Boi hardly had time to notice anything else going on around him all evening as he kept busy boxing the exploded grain and keeping the popper, butter-trough and salt shaker in production at top speed. People got hungry for popcorn as soon as they came within smelling distance. Before Boi got his first dozen boxes snapped shut and lined in a row along the glass windows of the machine, young and old carnival-goers started coming from all directions. Boi was barely aware of the spokes of sparkling lights on the Ferris wheel that turned dizzily into the sky and only faintly heard girls' screams that floated away like gay pennants into the night.

Nearby, the merry-go-round pumped out a wheezy tune that reminded Boi of the way his brother Edwin played the old foot pedal organ in the church basement. Loud as it was, the merry-go-round submerged into two dozen ballyhooers in front of tents, each with megaphone to mouth, assuring the crowd that flowed around rides and washed in waves along the shore of side shows that glittered with golden opportunities to win kewpie dolls by knocking stuffed figures off shelves with baseballs. Or they could win an ostrich feathered hat or red enameled cane at the shooting gallery where the silhouettes of wooden ducks marched mechanically across the back of a tent. Of course no one wanted to miss the chance of a lifetime to see the two-headed ape, or the girl who defied death by handling deadly snakes, or monkeys riding miniature cars so fast that the track had to have vertical sides.

Sights and sounds were lost on Boi the first night as he busily popped and boxed the snow. Evening dwindled into night and with it, the crowd. Popee shut down production and told Boi to be back by noon tomorrow.

Everything looked different in daytime. Boi hurried to the popcorn stand as the twelve o'clock siren wailed from the fire station. A few boys wandered around the tents and admired the huge carnival paintings of the tattooed lady, the snake charmer and the boxing champ who guaranteed to take on and lick all comers. A stream of people went in and out of the school building where judges dispensed ribbons for good, excellent and outstanding entries.

Popee was not in sight and the machine was cold. Boi nonchalantly sat in the little canvas folding chair under the big striped umbrella and gazed out at tent town, imagining himself to be the owner of the machine that, like some magical magnet, pulled money right out of the pockets of popcorn-hungry people.

His apron had pockets that held pennies, nickels, dimes and quarters. He discovered the night before that the apron had an inside pocket where money was kept to make big change.

Seeing a cleaning towel hanging on the side of the machine, Boi started polishing the glass and inside of the bin. By his second frame, Popee came by and lit the burner and told Boi to start boxing as soon as he had a hopper full. Boi wondered when the customers would start coming.

Many were in the school gym admiring the exhibits and picnickers were beginning to fill up the park across the street. He had scarcely boxed the first batch when motors were fired up and the rides began to move. The painted wooden horses began their smooth glide to a slow gallop on the merry-go-round's circular track accompanied by the hoots and whistles of the wheezing calliope music. As if coming right out of the ground a crowd gathered and Boi found himself selling popcorn almost as fast as he did night before.

During his busy preoccupation with keeping the machine in full production — perhaps it was late afternoon, he couldn't quite remember later — he became conscious of three picture-book girls staring at him! One was about his size, one about a head shorter and the third was very small. He felt certain he had seen them before somewhere as he returned their stares. Then he remembered.

Little, lacy-edged parasols were shouldered delicately behind flowered bonnets. Braided pig-tails with ribbon bows tied near the ends slid down the back of each girl. All three dresses were alike, with ruffles at the neck, sleeves and skirt. Each one wore a lace apron with a little pocket for a dainty handkerchief. Shoes matched shiny black patent leather purses that looked like they were right off the store shelf. Tops of half socks discreetly folded down showed embroidered flowers edged against a white that rivaled the popcorn in its purity. Boi wondered if they were on their way to a party. Except for their sizes, they could have been taken for triplets.

Rachael! Jenny! and Katy!

Rachael lowered her parasol and pointing it at him and said in her loudest, high thin voice, "There he is! There's that snake boy! Making popcorn, that's him! The snake boy!"

Jenny and Katy stared. Boi stared back.

"Two boxes, boy," said a booming voice and Boi was

jolted from his mesmerism. He absently handed two boxes in the direction of the voice and took the quarter in exchange, hardly moving his eyes from the girls. He was sure he had never seen any three girls who were as pretty as these. He recalled killing the rattler with them in the timber by Rock Creek earlier in the summer. He felt more acquainted with them than they were willing for him to be.

"Where's my change?" barked the voice.

"Oh, yes sir," said Boi handing him back a dime.

"Hey," said the voice to his companion, "they must be two fer fifteen this afternoon. Last night they wuz three fur a quarter." The comment was lost on Boi as his full attention was on his vision of loveliness.

"You're Katy, and Jenny and Rachael," he finally blurted out and immediately felt stupid since they knew who they were.

"I don't think we'd better get any popcorn," said Katy to her sisters.

"The snake boy is a carnie!" exclaimed Jenny and then repeated it as if not quite believing.

"We'd better tell Dad," said Rachael. "Come on, I'm going to tell Dad we found where the snake boy is." The three started to leave when Rachael let out a shriek. "I lost my dime!"

"That doesn't matter now," said Katy. "We'd better get to Dad right away." Her rising voice betrayed inner panic as Jenny and Katy dragged Rachael, sobbing and crying, away from the popcorn machine. Just before they were swallowed by the crowd of people, Boi noticed they headed for the park across the street. He tried to concentrate on the job before him but second, third and fourth thoughts crowded his mind. This encounter with the three ended the way it had before. They ran away with one of them crying. Why did he affect them this way, especially when he wanted to be friends? He remembered meeting them in the woods and their words… "Our Dad has two guns. One to shoot coyotes and one to shoot rustlers."

Boi nervously wondered if their Dad had his guns with him. They obviously had come to the fair for fun. Surely he wouldn't have brought guns with him. Anyway, why should he be nervous about guns — he was neither coyote nor rustler. Maybe he could take some popcorn over to them. The inspiration was interrupted by Popee who came bustling up to say, "I'll be gone a few minutes. Keep poppin' and keep sellin'. Gimme what you got in the till — keep a dollar's worth of change." Boi counted out a dollar and poured the remaining pockets of coins into Popee's cupped hands.

Maybe if he's gone long enough, Boi thought, I could run over to the park with three boxes of 'snow' — he was now into carnie jargon. I wonder if I could find them in that crowd — there must be a thousand folks over here. Grabbing three boxes, Boi ran ducking and dodging, around, in and through big and small groups, across the street and looked desperately for the three girls, not knowing what kind of family he might be looking for.

"There he is," shouted Jenny who spied Boi standing, looking in another direction, holding three boxes neatly flapped shut with butter stains coming through the sides. Six girls and two adults followed her pointing and all saw him at the same time. He turned and looked at them.

"Over here, son," said Mr. Eastman taking a few steps toward Boi who walked slowly toward the family picnic spot. His glance darted over the large blanket spread out on the ground with a smaller tablecloth in the middle. An open picnic basket had just given up its baked beans, potato salad, sandwiches and iced tea. No sight of a gun, Boi made a mental note almost expecting to see one.

"Son, are you the boy who picked up a rattler on my place and made it strike at the girls?"

"Yes sir. I mean, no sir. I mean it was dead," Boi said defensively.

"A dead rattler?" pressed Mr. Eastman.

"You can tell he's a carnie!" shouted Jenny pointing. "Look at his apron where he keeps money."

Boi looked down remembering his idea to give Rachael a dime for the one she lost. "I thought maybe that Katy and Jenny and Rachael would like some popcorn," he repeated feeling foolish.

"Son, how do you know the names of these girls?" again probed the rancher.

"They told me, well, not exactly, but when we were...when I was killing the snake, I heard them say so."

"We did not, Dad," declared Katy. "Did we Jenny, Rachael?"

"I think he's lying," said Jenny. "He's a carnie and carnies lie!"

"All right, Jenny," interrupted Mrs. Eastman.

"That's enough. People aren't liars until they're proven to be."

The case paused before judge and jury. Wide open eyes of the accusers returned the innocence of the wide open eyes of the accused. Boi shifted his footing and fingered the boxes of popcorn and suddenly remembered they were for the girls. He extended them in their direction.

"Don't take them," warned Rachael in her small voice,

now pitched higher than ever as she stepped back. "They're probably poisoned."

"No they aren't," countered Boi in his most conciliatory tone. "It's the same corn I've been popping all day. A lot of people would be dead by now if it had poison in it!" He then extended them to Mr. Eastman who made no move to accept the gifts.

Then Boi had an idea. If they didn't take the popcorn, maybe they would take the dime for the one Rachael lost. "Here's the dime Rachael lost. I found it on the ground." He reached in the dime pocket of his apron. As he felt the coin in his fingers, he was stricken by his double sin: he was both lying and taking money that didn't belong to him. Even as he held the coin to Rachael who darted to him and snatched it before it had time to be tainted by Boi's deceptions, he wondered if he would be struck dead for his deeds. But surely it isn't wrong to give something away, especially to a little girl in distress. Anyway, he was sure he could find the dime she dropped and return it to Mr. Popee. What about the popcorn he was so willing to give away? He could pay for that out of his wages for…but wait, maybe he wouldn't get any wages if Popee found him gone from the machine. He'd better get right back.

"Come here, young man," said Mrs. Eastman who

had been sitting on a corner of the blanket with legs crossed in front. She leaned forward to swing her knees together and sitting back, extended a hand to Boi. Boi took a few steps toward her but stopped short. "Come closer," she urged. "I want to look at your face."

Boi wondered what was wrong with his face or why she couldn't see him from where he stood. Mr. Eastman came to the pair and crouched on one knee with elbow on the other. The six Eastman daughters huddled close around the tablecloth to hear what their mother would say or what their father might do to Boi. Mrs. Eastman took the boxes of popcorn from Boi's nervous hands. She set them next to the jug of iced tea and taking Boi's hands in hers looked deeply into his eyes.

Boi thought of his mother, her eyes were like this woman's. He wondered if all mothers were as beautiful. His mother was beautiful, Boi had concluded long ago, because she was kind and fair about things and she seemed to understand so many strange and puzzling things that happened to a boy growing up in a baffling world. Mrs. Eastman was pretty and what she said made Boi feel at ease.

"That was nice of you to bring the girls some popcorn. I thank you for them. Do you live in Greenhills?"

"Yes ma'am, I do."

"Is your father the new Baptist preacher?" asked Mr. Eastman.

"Yes sir, he is." Boi retrieved his hands. He knew some people didn't like preachers.

"How'd you come to get this job?" pressed Mr. Eastman.

Boi recounted his experience with the carnival until he came to the part about Popee saying he'd be gone a few minutes and remembered with sudden panic that no one was at the machine. Without a word he spun and fled full speed, money apron bouncing off his legs.

"What do you think of that, Clara?" Mr. Eastman asked his wife.

"I think he's a good lad," she replied slowly, following the retreating boy with her eyes. "Only I wonder about the snake business — if it really was dead when he picked it up. I talked to Mrs. Smith and she said the Jacksons are good folks — nothing at all like the former preacher's family."

The smell of hot buttered popcorn went straight to the rancher's nose. "Go over and pay for this popcorn," said the rancher reaching in his pocket, "and get another five boxes."

"I don't want to go!" exclaimed Katy.

"Me neither!" echoed Jenny and Rachael.

"I will," brightened Mary. Now was her chance to get in on a little of the excitement she seemed to have missed.

"I'll go with her," eagerly chimed in Vivian who saw a chance to make a contact with the family she heard had a good looking older boy her age.

"If Vivian's going, I'll go," relented Katy.

Six Eastman girls marched double file in ranks of three across the street to the popcorn machine. As they approached, Jenny dropped Rachael's hand to go around a clump of people. Glancing at the ground, she saw a dime in the trampled grass and dirt. Picking it up, she realized that Boi had lied about the dime. Why would he lie? She hurried to catch up with her sisters now at the machine.

"Do you have an older brother?" she heard Vivian ask.

"Sure. Two of them," Boi answered.

Jenny noticed Mary came closer. "How old?"

"Seventeen and fifteen," came the answer that sent thrills shivering through seventeen and fifteen-year-old Vivian and Mary.

"Are they here at the Fair?" eagerly pressed Vivian.

"I don't know. . . haven't seen them. . . I s'pose they'll come sometime."

Jenny debated about confronting Boi about his lie. Maybe he was lying about having brothers, but he might not because her mother had said that Mrs. Smith told her there were five boys and one girl in the family.

She decided not to accuse him and would think about why he lied. He must have had some reason. After what he did to them with the snake, he surely must be a bad boy. Jenny was positive her mother was wrong about him. He had a reason that must be found out.

Jenny was not sure she could keep this secret. But maybe she could. Like most young girls, she had secrets that she had never told anyone, but she had two that she had only told her mother and one she had told only to her Dad and one each to Katy and Lucinda. Rachael revealed one of her secrets — she would never tell her another one.

As the six sisters moved away, Jenny glanced over her shoulder at Boi who stared after them, popcorn scoop in one hand, elbow propped against the machine. Boi gave a timid wave with a slight wrist motion of his free hand. Jenny felt a funny feeling inside that made her look back a second time.

After the family returned home and Jenny was alone with her mother in the kitchen, she whispered, "Mother, I want to tell you a secret."

Her mother crossed to the dining room door and closed it, then sat at the kitchen table. Jenny came close and reached into her apron pocket to produce the dime.

"I found this when we were going to the popcorn

machine where Rachael lost her dime. Now, do you see? The snake boy lied. He didn't find her dime. Doesn't that prove he's evil?"

Mrs. Eastman was quiet for awhile as she studied the dime Jenny held towards her. "It's wrong to lie. When people tell lies they're being evil. The Bible clearly tells us not to bear false witness. But I think the young lad — how do you know that's the dime Rachael lost? It could be another one that someone lost." Mrs. Eastman had long ago acquired the technique of a courtroom lawyer when trying to get information from her daughters.

"But mother, it was the exact same spot where Rachael lost her dime," insisted Jenny with rising anxiety to prove to her mother that she was wrong in her assessment of Boi's character. The confrontation put daughter against mother as young generations have always challenged the older's wisdom. One or the other must be proven right about the character of the real boy that stood behind that money-apron he had tied around him.

The challenge and response of every civilization in the long history of humankind lay just as surely in the outcome of that kitchen trial as in the most violent of battlefields. Jenny was sure she would be able to make her mother admit to error and thus crack her privileged position of unquestioned authority.

"Alright. Let's assume it is the one Rachael lost and let's assume Boi did lie about finding it. That still does not necessarily make him bad."

Jenny felt a flush of victory. She had maneuvered her mother into an admission the girls had never obtained from either parent. "So, do you mean," she asked round eyed with exaggerated inflection, "that it's sometimes alright to lie? Dad says it's never right to tell a lie." Now she could go to work on loosening the ethical system of her parents.

Clara Eastman knew she had to meet her child's question with a workable answer, but exactly how to tell her in a way that Jenny could understand would not be easy without destroying her entire belief in honesty. The older girls had never compelled the question in the way Jennifer now tested it.

"Jenny, sometimes people are forced to do things because they don't want to hurt someone. Maybe Boi thought he could help Rachael feel better by telling her he found her dime."

"But why couldn't he have said, 'Here Rachael, here's a dime for the one you lost.' Then he wouldn't have had to lie."

"Do you remember how badly you spoke to him —

called him a carnie and accused him of lying? He probably knew we wouldn't take anything from him with that attitude. He tried to give you some popcorn and you wouldn't take it. Actually, he was being generous with Rachael to give her his own dime."

"I'll bet that money wasn't his," retorted Jenny sensing she was not gaining on her argument with her mother, then, with a sudden inspiration, "I'll bet he stole that dime from the popcorn man! He lied and he stole! I'm sure he's evil!"

"Now just a minute, young lady. You're making a lot of assumptions you can't prove. Before you go any further, you'd better find out what you're talking about. Don't go around saying things you don't know for sure. That's the way gossip gets started and gossiping is as bad as lying."

🕉 🕉 🕉

"Two boxes o' corn." Popee handed over two boxes. "Ten cents a box…three for a quarter."

"Gimme three." Boi noticed Popee had only told him that snow sold for ten cents a box and that was the way Boi had been selling it. There must now be a discount, he surmised.

"Three boxes o' corn" came another voice. Popee

handed over three boxes.

"H'much?"

"Ten cents a box."

Boi watched Popee drop thirty cents in his apron and wondered why he didn't give the usual discount. Boi was about to tell him he had made a mistake when it occurred to him that that's how Popee did business. Boi decided not to ask him about it since Popee might think his error was exposing a shady way of dealing. Boi had the uneasy feeling Popee was not being quite honest. Popee noticed Boi puzzling about the transaction.

"There nuthin' wrong with it, lad. Some people just want two boxes. If you can coax them to buy one more at a special price, you got a deal. Other folks come in with a mind to buy three boxes to begin with. Ya don't need to coax 'em and the special's off fer that deal. See kid?"

"Yeah, guess I do," was Boi's non-committal response. "I hadn't thought of it that way," at least not until one big cow-puncher came by and asked for three and handed Popee a quarter without asking the price.

"Ten cents a box," said Popee. "I need another nickel."

"Whatcha mean?" bristled the cowhand. "Al said they wuz three fur a quarter."

"Ten cents a box," repeated Popee.

"Listen, ya little carnie-gypin' popcorn peddler. Ya ain't gonna charge me no ten cents a box when Al jus' come by and got three fer a quarter! Another thing, one more peep outta ya, and I'll stuff ya in that machine." The cowhand took his three boxes and picking up a fourth shook it at Popee. "This one's fer arguin' with me, see?"

Popee looked at Boi and shrugged, "Ya don't win 'em all." Exhibitors had long removed their prize winning quilts, bouquets of flowers, canned fruit and the ribbons that went with them. Even the free-spending, fun-loving, popcorn-eating carnival-goers began thinning out.

"Guess I won't need ya no more," said Popee. "Here's a dollar and half: fifty cents fer last night and a dollar fer t'day."

The big dollar bill covered Boi's open hand and the heavy half dollar felt like his Dad's glass paperweight. As he started to go, Boi hesitated, turned back. "I owe you ten cents out of this," he blurted holding the fifty-cent piece toward Popee.

"Whatcha mean? If ya ate a box of snow, fergit it."

"No, I gave a dime to a little girl."

Popee looked at him closely. "Ya mean ya gave my money away?" he asked sternly.

Boi's insides went soft. He wished he hadn't told Popee

— just asked for five dimes and then left one on the machine — too late now. "A little girl wanted a box of popcorn, but she lost her dime. So I gave her one."

Popee took Boi's half dollar, returning four dimes and ten cents worth of advice. "Lissen, kid. Don't give no girl nothin'. They're all alike and a big pack of trouble, see? Jus' don't fool around with 'em. Keep clear away frum them, son, an' you'll be a lot better off, see?"

"Yes, sir. Well, I gotta go." Boi hurried away and felt cleansed of his guilt. Walking along the darkened sidewalks under the lofty elms that smudged street light shadows across lawns and walks, Boi was aching tired. With his left hand he felt the neatly folded dollar bill in his overall pocket, and in his right hand the four honest dimes. He was rich! In the block before the corner to go home, his pace slowed to match the tiredness that walked with him.

Was Popee really right? Are girls a big batch of trouble? They seemed to be a problem to Boi anyway. He wanted to be friends with Rachael, Jenny and Katy, but why did they always end up running away? Of course they had a right to when he scared them with the rattler. They sure were pretty, he thought. School would start next week. Maybe Katy would be in his class. He was sure if she got acquainted with him they could become good friends.

He liked their mother. She was pretty and made him feel good when she talked to him. He wasn't sure about their Dad. Boi got the feeling that he didn't trust him any more than the girls did. He was glad Rachael took his dime even though he was untruthful about it. And they all did come over and buy eight boxes of "snow" — Boi didn't like the carnie word of "snow" and spit it out of his mind. Six girls and all dressed alike. Boi had never seen a family like that. Rachael, Jenny and Katy were only half the children in the family. He was glad to find that out. People sometimes made comments about his big family. Now it didn't seem so big.

Boi wished his sister were more his age then maybe she'd tell him how girls thought. A light was still on in the dining room. Upstairs in the corner bedroom, some yellow light filtered out of the window and played off large sycamore leaves on a branch that touched the house. His brothers must be going to bed, he thought.

His mother sat at the dining room table piled high with the week's washing. A three-bulb chandelier hung from the ceiling over the table. The light seemed dim by comparison to the carnival. Boi sat wearily in a chair and told his mother everything that happened during the day, including Popee's parting advice.

"Sounds like Mr. Popee has had a bad time somewhere in his life," said Boi's mother. "No, girls are not just a 'big batch of trouble.' Oh, of course bad girls can be trouble for anyone, but then, so can bad boys. People are good or bad because of the way they are or the kind of home life they had growing up. You should beware of bad men just as much as bad women. I don't know about the girls you saw. Sounds like they come from a good family. You'll probably find out about them when school starts."

The next morning, Boi wandered over to the football field. He was amazed to see that all the tents were gone and the rides were being dismantled. He went to the spot where the popcorn machine had been. The grass was trampled smooth. A little patch was bare where the machine had been. Boi leaned against a tree and looked over the field. As he glanced down at the flattened grass, he saw a quarter almost at his feet. It must have fallen out of Popee's pocket, he thought. He sure couldn't give it back now. He didn't have the slightest idea where Popee came from or where he went.

IV

The Annual Picnic Fair disappeared from the football field and out of the gym as if by magic. That signaled doors to swing open for school's start in the Fall. The schoolhouse bell rang out, calling reluctant students from all directions, much to their parent's great relief. Wood floors smelled of fresh linseed oil, washed windows sparkled in bright morning sunshine, clean blackboards with chalk and erasers in their troughs at the ready and the American flag outside, snapping in a rising morning wind.

Boi and Frankie walked a respectful distance behind Edwin and Wilfred who didn't want to be seen with their younger brothers. "Get lost," commanded Wilfred. "We don't want to look like a squad of ducks marching into school."

New pupils, mostly first graders didn't know where they should go but a tall teacher gathered her brood at the intersection of two hallways. Frankie gave a look of misgiving at his disappearing brothers, but slowly followed the group of his size children to a classroom around the corner.

It didn't take Boi long to find his room that had a number posted above the door. He could hear a buzz of conversation as he entered and saw that the seats were nearly full. He wished his mother would have meals more promptly so he wouldn't be late. The teacher saw him standing in the doorway looking around for a seat in the back of the room.

"We have a desk up here," she said as the entire class turned to inspect the new student. "I believe you are Boi Jackson, aren't you?"

"Yes Ma'am," ears turning red as he heard several snickers and some under-the-breath comments as he walked to the front and slid into an empty seat.

"Boy Jackson! Sure a good thing he wasn't a girl," was a quiet but audible whisper. Then another hoarse whisper that Boi was sure the teacher heard, but chose to ignore it. "Baby boy Jackson. Just call me BB!" and snickering rippled across the room among the boys.

"BB is for bird brain," one of the larger boys pronounced and the ripple became loud enough that the teacher called the class to order and looked straight at George who was often the source of disruption. The teacher had been warned about George by his previous teacher. Order was restored and the whispering and giggling ceased.

The teacher explained what books and supplies each

pupil would need to bring the next day. Instructions continued about music classes and recesses together with raised hand signals for excusings. They were also told the way class was to be dismissed — same as last year. The teacher also promised to read a chapter from a favorite book each day if it went well and everyone studied their lessons. Boi liked the teacher at first sight and was sure he was going to like this year at school. A bell sounded in the hallway and the teacher announced time for recess.

"Hands on desk," said the teacher as she looked over the class for compliance.

"Turn,

"Stand,

"Pass."

At that signal, each row formed a single file and walked through the door under the watchful eye of the teacher who made sure there was no pushing or talking. The file of students went down the steps and marched out of the building where they stood in line on the wide sidewalk at their designated spot. When they were dismissed, pandemonium broke loose amid screams of girls and yells of boys making a dash to swings, teeter-totters, volleyballs, relay races and assorted games.

Boi hung back to look over what he could do that

would be the least conspicuous, but he wasn't going to be allowed to be obscure. Two boys, one taller and one shorter, sauntered toward him. The taller one said in a voice that was half accusing and half sarcastic, "Yer tha' new preachur's kid, aintcha'?"

"Yeah," answered Boi as he noticed he was being inspected for muscles and tested for courage. The tone of voice made Boi sure that some people didn't like preachers. Boi didn't know the taller boy was top cock in the sixth grade. He was making sure that Boi was not a threat to his status.

"Wanna fight?" asked the taller as two more boys drifted to the threesome. Boi sensed hostility and had the sinking feeling they were all going to jump him. He wondered why they wanted to fight. It seemed stupid to him and he said so.

"Lissen, kid. Nobuddy calls me stupid and gets away wit it, see? Jes don' cause me no trubble," said the taller boy giving Boi a push. Boi hadn't noticed the shorter boy had gotten on his hands and knees behind him. The push sent Boi sprawling on his back over the crouched boy. Laughter and fingers pointing at him reddened his ears for the second time that morning. He felt foolish as he got up and brushed himself off. "Jus don't give me no trubble, see," said Boi's unknown tormenter again, shaking his fist in Boi's face, "or I'll let ya have this in your snout!"

"I'm not trying to give anybody any trouble," replied Boi as he walked toward the building amid the jeers of the boys. Third graders playing touch tag ran into him and yelled at him to watch where he was going. He was about to decide school was not a friendly place when two girls walked in front of him and stopped — facing him. They stood for a minute looking at him.

"Aren't you the snake boy?"

"Katy!" exclaimed Boi, temporarily forgetting his recent humiliation at the Fair, and regaining his courage at the memory of killing a rattler in front of her and her sisters. "Do you go to school here?" blurted Boi and as soon as he said it realized how silly his question was. "I mean, what grade are you in?"

"Oh, Pattie and I are in the same room as you. If you'd ever turn around you'd see us."

𝒟 𝒟 𝒟

One day after school, Boi was walking home, watching his shadow on the sidewalk and thinking about a poem he read called, "Me and My Shadow."

As he walked, he heard muffled voices of some boys behind him. From the corner of his eye, he saw one shadow creeping towards his back. He suspected a trick. Just as the shadow moved to leap upon him, he made a quick side step and George went sprawling face down on the sidewalk.

"Lissen, kid," George jumped up. "I'm gonna knock yer block off!" and he began beating Boi with doubled fists. Boi raised his hands to ward off the blows. He noticed that George had skinned his face and it was beginning to bleed. Other boys began to circle around to watch the commotion. George was pummeling Boi with his fists and Boi was trying to back away from his reach. Just as George was about to land a haymaker into Boi's face, a strong arm grabbed George by the neck and lifted him off his feet.

"What do you think you're doing," the big boy yelled, grabbing George by the arm.

"He made me fall down," George said lamely. By this time a few drops of blood ran down George's face looking like they were coming from his nose.

"Did you hit him?" was the stern voice of Edwin.

"No, he was hitting me," stoutly declared Boi.

"Then how did he get the bloody nose?"

"Off the sidewalk, I guess." Edwin looked at Boi and turned loose of George's arm.

"You'd better run home and get your mother to take care of that before you bleed to death. Come on, Boi let's go." The two walked the few blocks home while Boi gave his brother a detailed account of what happened. "Why did George pick on you?" asked Edwin.

"Don't know," said Boi and then related what George had told him at recess several days before.

"He's the class bully," surmised Edwin. "There's one in every class — wants to make sure everyone knows he's king of the mountain."

Boi avoided George whenever he could but at times when he couldn't, George would double his fists and glare at Boi muttering, "I'm gonna git ya, Boi." By this time, word had passed that the big boy that grabbed George by the collar was one of Boi's older brothers. Not only that, Boi had *two* older brothers. This restrained the sixth grade boys from any further physical or verbal abuse of Boi.

On Saturdays when the weather was good, Boi wandered to the school grounds and exercised on the playground equipment. He especially liked the chains that hung from a center pole and had two handles to hang onto. He could run in a circle and lift his feet off the ground, swinging in a large arc while hanging onto the handles. There were eight chains with handles and when eight boys were on them it was more fun because they could make them go faster and in wider circles, like the swinging rides at the Fair.

After a few running jumps, Boi was becoming winded and went over to the swings. Sitting in one, he wound himself up, then lifting his feet, spun around as the swing unwound. He had done this only three times when he heard someone say, "You'll make yourself dizzy doing that."

He opened his eyes and saw Katy standing nearby. "Katy! What are you doing here?" he exclaimed.

"The folks came to town with Vivian and Lucinda so I thought I'd tag along — nice day." Katy sat in a swing next to Boi.

"Did you hear what happened to George two weeks ago?" asked Boi.

"He came to school with a bandage on his forehead, I noticed. He said he ran into a post at Mr. Horndecker's shop."

"He's not only the bully for sixth graders but he doesn't tell the truth, either," Boi noted. "That's not what happened, " said Boi who then went on to relate how George skinned his forehead.

"That's certainly a different story than what he told Pattie and me," said Katy. "I thought it was fishy. Served him right for jumping on you. A person would have to be blind to run into a post at Mr. Horndecker's shop. I'd better run," she said abruptly. "My folks said to meet them at the grocery store in half an hour. They warned me not to be late."

"Wait. I'll go with you. It's on my way home," said Boi as they left the swings. They had not reached the sidewalk when they heard a crash of broken glass. "Did you hear that?" asked Boi.

"Yes. It sounded like it came from the back of the school," said Katy.

Just then a boy came running around the building and headed up the street away from them.

"Look!" said Katy. "There goes Luke Collins. He's in high school and I heard he gets into lots of trouble."

"Let's go see," said Boi.

"I can't. It's late and Dad will be angry if I'm late."

The two walked toward town just as the shop teacher drove by and waved to them. They noticed he drove around the building on the dirt road that led to the back of the building and ended at the large door to the shop. At the same time, they noticed George and one of his buddies going onto the playground but when the shop teacher's car approached the school, George and his friend ran off.

"Well, we missed good old George," said Boi with relief.

"He never has liked me since the first day. I wonder why that it is. Edwin says it's because he wants to be 'top dog' and if anyone threatens his being that, he resents it."

On Monday morning, the reading class was interrupted by the principal coming to the door and motioned for the teacher. "Do you have George Patterson in your class?"

"Yes," she said pointing him out.

"Tell him to come to the office," he said as he walked away. After George had gone, Boi turned and gave a knowing look to Katy who nodded. George was gone a long time. When they were all outside during recess, Boi asked Katy if she had any idea what George had done.

"Do you suppose it had anything to do with the glass we heard Saturday?" he speculated.

"Maybe it did," she said. "Let's ask the teacher." When they told the teacher what they saw and heard on Saturday they did not think George was involved, the teacher said she would investigate the matter.

When the class returned, the teacher told them to take out their arithmetic books and work on an assigned exercise. She would be gone briefly and would check their work when she got back. George was still not back and the class began to whisper that he must be in deep trouble. When she returned she assigned students to put problems on the board leaving out Boi and Katy. They were to report to the office.

On opening the office door, they heard the shop teacher asking George why he ran off when he drove around to the shop door.

"I don't know why — guess I thought you would get after me fer bein' on the playground."

"Now George, you know that's not a good reason. If you didn't break that window, you would not have had any reason to run."

At that moment Boi and Katy came into the office. The principal said the teacher told him what Boi and Katy had said.

"Did George break the glass?" asked the principal.

Boi looked at Katy who made a gesture urging him to tell what they saw.

"I don't think George broke the window. Katy and I were sitting on the swings and were leaving when we heard the sound of breaking glass. Then this boy…"

"And I know who he is," interrupted Katy. It was Luke Collins!" The announcement struck silence.

The principal cleared his throat. "How do you know he did it?"

"Well, we didn't *see* him do it," said Boi," but we heard

the breaking glass and then saw him run away at the far end of the building. We had walked halfway to town when Mr. Wirth drove by and turned to see George and another boy on the playground. We didn't see him run away but we did hear the breaking glass *before* he walked onto the ground."

The principal looked at Mr. Wirth who returned the look. "Well, we'd better get Luke down here. You three can go back to your class."

On the way back, George said, "Thanks fer what ya done fer me. They were goin' to expel me fer not tellin' the truth."

"But it was the truth," said Boi.

"It sure was," said Katy.

"My Dad says to always tell the truth," continued Boi. "The consequences for lying are always worse."

🕊 🕊 🕊

Boi had managed to get his breakfast down in a hurry so he was at school before class started.

"I heard in church yesterday you are going to play in a recital on Saturday afternoon," Boi eagerly told Katy Monday morning before she had time to put new pencils in her pencil box.

"Oh she would," groaned Katy. "I don't see why my teacher has to tell everyone about it!"

"Why, what's so bad about recitals?"

"They make me nervous!" Katy gave a shudder.

"Mrs. Streit said she had some very excellent pupils," said Boi intending to give some encouragement.

"She's always telling us that but it doesn't keep me from getting nervous," wailed Katy.

"Do very many people come?"

"All the proud Daddys and Mothers and kids too young to stay at home by themselves. People are all over the place."

"How long have you been taking lessons?" Boi was curious.

"Seems like all my life," Katy said.

"I'll bet you're good." Then he added, "Think I'll come."

"You'd better not," hissed Katy holding her pencils like sharp daggers. "I'll never, ever speak to you again if you do."

By the end of the week, Katy threatened Boi with every form of instant annihilation her mind could conceive if he appeared at the recital and, not only that, she would have her Dad bring his guns and stand at the door to keep Boi out.

Saturday found Boi and his mother as eager spectators

in the Methodist Church. Boi's mother was a good pianist and was trying to help her five sons to at least learn the notes on the keyboard.

The church was nearly half full, "a good turnout for a recital," said Mrs. Streit who thanked all who were present. The parents, brothers, sisters, aunts, uncles, and grandparents of the performers sat whispering to one another and it made Katy think it was more like a funeral instead of a recital.

Parents speculated on whether they would witness great humiliation of their child ("I'm sure Suzie will not do well, she doesn't practice enough") or if there would be an electrifying discovery of a keyboard genius uncovered by Mrs. Streit's patience. The program started with younger pupils astonishing their parents with performances of "Flying Fingers" and "Wooden Shoes," followed by advanced beginners playing slightly more complex, "Blue Fountain," "Venetian Boat Song," and "Drifting Stars." It culminated in semi-professional levels of performances by advanced students playing compositions by Schubert, Brahms and Chopin.

Katy finished her rendition of Chopin's "Etude" with a few flaws but she covered them well and they went unnoticed by the unpracticed ears of the listeners. There was enthusiastic applause and none more loud than Boi who was immensely impressed and he told her so during the reception that followed. She was blushing from the many compliments given by many other parents who told her they hoped their child would be able to do as well someday.

※ ※ ※

One year followed another and increasingly, Boi enjoyed Katy's companionship. Even George's attitude changed by the time they were in high school. George would often walk "to town" with the two of them when Katy went there to meet her ride home with her sisters.

"Mother, let's invite Boi to Sunday dinner," said Katy one day after school. "Now that Vivian has gone to the University, he could sit in her place at the table," she suggested.

"I suppose we could," replied Mrs. Eastman then added, "Do you remember when you, Jenny and Rachael said he was evil?"

"Oh, Mother, that was a long time ago. Besides, we found out he had only played a bad trick on us." They both laughed at the memory.

At school the next day, Katy came running through the

hall to Boi's locker and asked if his folks would let him come out for dinner next Sunday.

"I think they would. I don't know why they wouldn't. I'll ask them when I get home."

Sunday came and Katy was excited. She took extra pains to brush her hair and see that her dress was just right. The Eastmans always went to the Methodist Church every "Lord's Day" as soon as Dad Eastman could change into his Sunday suit after milking their two cows.

"Hurry up, Katy," called her mother. "We're all waiting."

When the church service was over, the seven Eastmans climbed into their car and waited for Boi.

"Maybe the Baptists had one of their long services," commented Mr. Eastman. "I've noticed they sometimes carry on for a good while longer than we do."

At that moment, Boi rounded the corner of the church and started to enter the car through the open rear door. As he stepped on the running board he stopped to see Jenny sitting backwards behind the front seat. He had seen the long sedan before, but had never ridden in it.

"It's alright. Jenny will let you in," laughed Katy. "It gets a bit crowded when we're all in. You can sit back here."

"I didn't know you had little seats like that," said Boi as he settled in next to Katy and looked at the jump seats

Jenny and Rachael were on. "How do you like riding backwards?" Boi asked Jenny.

"It's fun. We get to see the faces of everyone in the back seat!" chirped Rachael.

"Oh, and we can see out of the windows real good," said Jenny. Just as she said that the car came to a sudden stop.

"Look out for old Bossie!" exclaimed Mrs. Eastman.

"Now how did she get out on the road?" bellowed Mr. Eastman in great exasperation as he punched the brake pedal, pitching the back seaters into the jump seaters. Opening his door, Mr. Eastman jumped out and started chasing their choice milk cow down the road. Bossie turned, ran for the ditch and back toward the car. Boi thought he could help and jumped out of the back seat, waving his arms at the approaching cow. She headed straight for Boi.

Boi kept waving his arms, shouting "Whoa, Bossie," but Bossie didn't get the message and kept coming. Boi decided he'd better get out of the way of a half-ton bovine but as he stepped aside, tripped and fell into the dusty road in his Sunday best.

Katy jumped out to see if Boi was hurt but the other girls and Mrs. Eastman were enjoying the spectacle of the chase. Boi jumped to his feet and dusted himself and followed Katy's Dad in pursuit of old Bossie, yelling to her to come back. As soon as Bossie heard Katy's shrill command, the cow stopped, turned around and meekly returned to Mr. Eastman who grabbed her around the neck and scolded the cow. But when Katy came to her, she tickled Bossie's ear and whispered into it, a calming trick she had learned from her older sisters.

By this time, Mr. Eastman saw where the fence had been down and guided Bossie back through it into the field. Making a temporary repair, he returned to the car, saying he would take them home than come back for a better fix.

"But what if she comes back?" wailed Rachael.

"She won't. I gave her a whack on the rump and she took off for the lower pasture. She won't come back before I do."

Katy helped Boi dust himself off and all three climbed back into the car and rode to the house.

Later at dinner, after Mr. Eastman had changed his clothes and repaired the fence, Mary joked that if Boi had a red cape he would make a good Spanish toreador. Everyone laughed except Katy who felt responsible for the welfare of her invited guest.

"That's not very funny. Suppose Boi had fallen on a rock and hit his head!"

"I don't think it could have hurt me," said Boi. "I have

a pretty hard head, or at least that's what my Dad says." And everyone laughed again to know Boi's feelings were not hurt as bad as his Sunday clothes.

"Why do you suppose Katy had such an influence on old Bossie?" posed Mr. Eastman.

"Because she's a girl," said Rachael giggling.

"Do you mean to say she doesn't like us men?" asked her Dad.

Laughter.

Dinner was over and the dishes were done. Mr. Eastman took his Sunday nap and Katy said, "Lets go to the woods and see if our tepee is still up."

Boi and the three girls went trooping to the clearing where they first met. "Yup, it's still here. After you scared us we came back and fixed the tepee. Only this time, we made it with four sticks." said Jenny.

"Why did you scare us with that rattler?" Katy asked Boi.

"Oh, I don't know," replied Boi. "But I did feel really bad when I made Rachael cry."

"Yeah, you really did scare me," declared Rachael.

"Me too," Jenny rejoined.

"We couldn't figure out how you knew our names," Katy said quizzically, still wondering.

"I don't remember exactly," said Boi, going to the same

broken branch where he sat dreaming only a few years before. Closing his eyes he said contemplatively, "but I think Jenny said, 'Katy, he's going to use your pole,' when I went for the snake with Katy's stick. Then at one time, Katy told Rachael to step back. When Jenny heard the snake's rattle, Katy said that Jenny was right. I then had all three of your names," said Boi triumphantly as he felt a flush of pride at his memory. Of course he had rehearsed the incident many times since it happened and carefully remembered their names for any future need.

While he sat with his eyes closed, Katy motioned to the others to follow her quietly to the other side of Boi and at her signal, all three let loose with blood curdling screams. Boi jumped and nearly fell off the branch. Startled, he thought there must be another snake somewhere. "Where's the snake?" he asked.

"Right behind you," yelled Katy, echoed by Jenny and Rachael. Boi turned and jumped toward them, tripping on part of the branch and falling on the ground toward them.

"He's crawling up your pant leg," yelled Jenny.

By this time, Boi saw the laughing faces of his tricksters as they danced around him, then grabbing his hand pulled him into a line and they danced playfully around the tepee.

As Boi recalled his Sunday with the Eastmans that night

at home, his mind and emotions raced with beautiful images of the three sisters and wished he could have been their big brother. Frankie was all right but he was nothing like the girls. But as he thought about Katy, he thought maybe she could be more than a sister…

D D D

One evening in spring, before the grass greened, Boi was riding his bicycle. As he rode toward the east out of town, he noticed the sky seemed red. That's strange, he thought. The sun was setting to his back so why was there a red glow in the east?

Boi rode up a trail that led to a high point from which he could look out toward the glow. What he saw from the top, he could not believe! From the southeast to the east and the northeast there was a great rim of fire. In some places the line of fire burned down a slope like some giant mouth drooling fire down its lower lip. He had heard something about how the end of the world would come in fire. Even as he watched he saw far down the valley men on horseback riding furiously with firebrands toward the crest of another hill. The spectacle made him think of the four horsemen of the Apocalypse. He didn't stay long to watch the world being consumed but rushed back in the fast-fading light to tell his father what he had seen.

"No," said his Father. "The ranchers are burning off the pasture. They do it each year to kill pests and weeds and diseases that would affect the grass. After a few rains, the grass returns – greener then ever and fattens the cattle for market."

"But what about the horsemen with fire brands?" insisted Boi. "You told us one time about the 'Four Horsemen of the Apocalypse.'"

"They were probably starting back fires to stop the advance of the fire. You may have noticed there was hardly any wind which made it possible to contain the burning."

Boi went to bed that night with dreams of a world conflagration and flames licking at the bottom of his house.

***

At school, Katy told Boi that they heard from her big sister, Vivian, who was at the university. It seems that Vivian had found a young man who was studying law and, "…she has been going on dates with him," said Katy with excitement.

"Do you suppose they're serious?" asked Boi.

"I don't know, but Lucy and Mary are sure looking forward to going. Lucy will go next year and Mary the year after that."

"Then it will be your turn?" surmised Boi.

"Sure. Dad says he wants all of his girls to get an education whether they're married or not."

"I guess if you graduate and don't get married you'll become a teacher, or nurse, or telephone operator, or something," observed Boi.

"I heard of one woman who went on to become a doctor," said Katy. "But I think I would rather be married than be a doctor."

"Then why would you want to go to college?" pressed Boi. "My mother never went nor did yours. I think they're pretty good mothers. I wouldn't think mothers would need college."

"Well, Dad says that college helps mothers better understand how to rear children and help them when they're sick, and help manage the family finances, and…oh, lots of things," declared Katy.

"I suppose so," said Boi as he turned that thought over in his mind.

"And besides," continued Katy, "he says that times are changing and things aren't like they were when he was young."

That put Boi on another track. He thought of Greenhills. Would it ever change? Would Mr. Horndecker's blacksmith shop always be there? He imagined Main Street getting paved like those in the county seat. And Hilton's grocery and Smitty's Service Station. What would Greenhills look like when the times changed? The train station and railroad would surely be there. The one passenger train a day that stopped in the morning to pick up the people going one way, like Vivian when she went off the college, and the one in the evening that brought people back, and the freight trains that didn't stop unless they let off cattle cars that were filled and later hauled away —- Boi couldn't imagine that ever changing.

But life flows in one direction. Like the spring-fed stream that meandered past the hills and made the woods grow in the valley around Greenhills, Boi wondered where it came from and where it went. He was to find out.

𝔇 𝔇 𝔇

The Baptist preacher was not accepted by all the members of his congregation. There were some who thought he was too "modern," as they called it. One old deacon who had rigid ideas about what should be preached from the pulpit, they should be "straight out of the Bible," as he put it.

One Sunday morning, Rev. Jackson read a passage from the Book of Psalms that asked, "What is man that thou art mindful of him?" The subject of his sermon dealt with the vastness of God and His universe. Man is just a speck on the earth and the sun is so far away that it takes almost ten minutes for light to come ninety-three million miles from it to the earth.

The next day, the crusty old deacon met him in the corner bank and said in a combative voice that dripped with sarcasm, "Parson, how'd ja' know it's ninety-three million miles to tha sun? It don't say so in th' Bible!"

"You're absolutely right, Brother Deacon. I didn't get that information out of the Bible."

"I s'pose you got it from one of them atheist science books," sneered the Deacon.

"I wouldn't say, 'atheistic'," Rev. Jackson replied. "Science books don't go into the subject of God."

"That 's what I mean. You're s'posed to preach 'bout what's in the word of God, not what's the word of science."

"Let me ask you this: Do you believe in God the Almighty?"

"Of course I do but what's that got to do with it?"

"Does that mean God created everything?" asked the reverend.

"Sure, but what's that got to do with the Bible?"

"Well, if God created everything, the earth and all that's in and around it, the sun and moon and stars, what's so wrong about astronomers studying what God created?"

But the deacon was not satisfied. The Bible was the sacred Word of God and preachers were supposed to confine their preaching strictly to what's in it. The old deacon took a dislike to Rev. Jackson and his "modernism." He accused the pastor of mixing a lot of "atheistic science" stuff with the Bible and he wasn't demur about sharing his opinion about this man of the cloth.

It wasn't long before he had the congregation in an uproar over the preacher and enough folks agreed with the Deacon that Rev. Jackson was asked to find another congregation.

𝕯 𝕯 𝕯

The small graduation class met for the last time in the school auditorium.

Very few planned to go on to college. Three of the boys were going to work on their dad's ranch. Two of the girls were getting married and one was taking a job in the grocery store. Boi and Katy had discussed their futures many times during the last year.

"Dad said I should go on to the university. I'll be his fourth daughter to get a higher education. When he and mother talk to other folks, I hear Dad say, 'Yep, we have six daughters. Three in college and three more to go!' He's proud that we've all been good students."

"You would have been valedictorian if I hadn't outscored you in math and chemistry," said Boi, somewhat apologetically.

"Well I don't care. I didn't like math and I wouldn't have taken chemistry if Dad hasn't insisted. He said a person ought to know a little bit about everything, especially when they get to college. Anyway, I'm glad you were valedictorian instead of George."

"George has turned out to be a pretty good guy," observed Boi. "The way we started out, I wasn't sure we'd ever be friends."

"He's been talking about taking pharmacy in college so he can take over his dad's drugstore some day," said Katy.

"Yeah, he mentioned that to the chemistry teacher a lot, but you saw how he wasn't very good at the subject."

"So what are you going to do now that your dad is

having to move?" Katy asked what everybody in town was wondering.

Boi smiled. He knew two things he wasn't supposed to tell Katy — at least just yet. He diverted a direct answer by saying, "Maybe your dad can take me on, at least for the summer. He might be able to use another ranch hand."

"Oh that would be great!" exclaimed Katy with excitement. Then, thinking out loud, "There's room for two more in the bunkhouse."

That evening at supper, Mrs. Eastman mentioned that she heard the Jacksons were moving to Williamstown. Both Wilfred and Edwin were in college but what would Boi do. "Maybe you could use him on the ranch?" asked Katy a bit timidly, looking at her Dad who saw the same look in his daughter's eyes he had seen many times in his wife's when she had made suggestions in a tone to avoid controversy.

"Do you think he would be interested?" asked the rancher.

"I think so. At least, well, I don't think he knows what he will do when his dad leaves. He did say he plans to go to college, eventually."

Mr. Eastman smiled with the look he sometimes gave his family when he was harboring some great secret.

"Alright," chided Mrs. Eastman. "Whose canary did

you swallow?"

"I already asked him and he will be here for the summer."

"Oh, Daddy!" said Katy as she threw her arms around him. His unshaven, scratchy face never felt so good. Then, suddenly realizing Boi knew when she asked him what he was gong to do in the summer, she pouted, "Why didn't he tell me you asked him, mother?" Katy demanded. "Do men keep secrets from women?"

"Yes, and vice versa," smiled Mrs. Eastman.

"Only sisters have secrets," put in Jenny as the room filled with lyrical laughter that was so often heard in the Eastman dining room.

"One of the first things you need to learn is how to saddle Ole Buster," said Mr. Eastman as he showed Boi the routine of throwing on the saddle, tightening the belly strap and putting on the bridle. Boi caught on fast and was soon riding Buster around the barnyard with the confidence of a seasoned cowhand.

"Buster's a good horse," he told Boi. "The girls have ridden him a lot and he's gentle and responsive. He almost knows what you want to do before you do."

Soon, horse and rider became one and Boi's job was as pleasant to him as it was exhausting. One of the first chores Mr. Eastman gave him was riding the fences. There were places that needed mending, where fence posts were rotted and needed replacing. In other places, the barbed wire was sagging and needed restringing. This was an important part of the work, he was told, since the cattle had to be kept from wandering into someone else's pasture or, worse, getting out on the road.

On one of his rides along the fences, Boi came across a post with a shallow hole rotted in the middle into which a bluebird had built its nest. The bluebird flew off as Boi approached on Buster. Looking into the nest at four pale blue eggs, Boi decided to not disturb the nest since the post appeared to be fairly firm otherwise and would certainly hold until after the birds were hatched and gone.

A bit further along the fence he saw a meadowlark perched on the wire, singing its "cheer-i-le-eo." As it flew away another bird fluttered up from the grass and flew off. Approaching the spot, Boi looked down to see the meadowlark's nest with eggs in it. Each egg carried in it new life that would become a bird, thought Boi. How many eggs must be in this vast pasture?

Stopping Buster, Boi looked over the endless sea of grass and in the sun-warmed breeze thought maybe the life of a rancher might be for him. Then he thought about Katy. What if Katy went to college and found someone else that she liked better than him? He had a sinking feeling that darkened his thoughts about Katy. She was more than just a good friend now. He was beginning to have romantic thoughts about her and the idea that she would go off with some other fellow ignited a spark of possessive jealousy.

The summer was another hot one but long evenings were cool enough for Boi and Katy to have serious conversations about going to school and the array of adventures and opportunities spreading out before them. Vivian, Lucy and Mary were home for the summer, bringing the Eastman family up to full strength. Vivian was eager to tell everyone about the boy she was getting serious with. After two years she was sure he was the one for her.

"Has he proposed to you?" asked Lucy.

"Well, sort of. He graduates next spring and says he hopes I'll come with him to a job he's been offered in Centerville."

"That's not much of a proposal," put in Mary. "I think he ought to come right out and ask you to marry him…give you an engagement ring."

Boi and Lucy were listening intently to Vivian's account of her dates with Bob, her latest and best crush. They were all out in the yard. Boi sat astride the top of the big tire swing Mr. Eastman made for the girls when they were small.

Katy sat in the tire idly moving it around. Turning to Boi, Lucy asked what he had heard from Edwin and Wilfred. Lucy had become more than casually interested in Wilfred when the Jacksons lived in Greenhills.

"Mother wrote that they are staying at school for the summer. They found jobs that will help them get through another year."

"Do you plan to go to school next fall?" asked Vivian.

"I don't know...not sure my employer will let me," said Boi to the laughter of the girls.

"Tell him to raise your wages," said Mary.

"Yeah, yeah, yeah," chorused the girls.

Boi had already calculated that a dollar a day plus room and board wouldn't get him very far into a semester at college. Of course, he could hunt for a job like Edwin and Wilfred did, but that would be iffy. Besides, he would like to have enough to go through the first year without being pressured to find and hold down a job. That way, he could concentrate on his studies.

With all three of the girls back for the summer the house was again full of laughing, giggling, and occasionally, a squeal from the bedrooms. Boi was necessarily consigned to the bunkhouse where he got acquainted with Fred and Pete, who created a far different domestic ambience.

Pete was a floater who came into town looking for a job as a cow puncher. He was a loner and had little to say. He did reveal that he was from Texas and had plenty of experience driving herds. Mr. Eastman found him at Mr. Horndecker's blacksmith shop. He traveled light with a small bag containing clothes and toiletries on the back of a horse called Star, for the white marking on its forehead. His dark leathery face showed deep creases from his life outdoors in the elements, premature for his thirty years. His sweat-stained, ten-gallon hat was frayed and as faded as his chaps that showed wear from hard riding.

Fred, on the other hand, was outgoing, played a guitar and sang a lot of songs. His hat was new, as were his other clothes. Boi wondered at the difference between the two men. After a few nights in the bunkhouse he learned that Fred was the same age as Pete but was looking for "a woman." "They come in mighty handy," he told Boi.

"On the other hand," Pete told Boi, "they was nuthin' but trouble." He had "a woman" once. They had a child but "she tuk tha kid an' run away with all my money."

"Butcha better look out, Boi. If'n ya look cross-eyed at wun of Dad Eastman's girls you'll git yer walkin' papers reel quik!" For all his reticence, Pete was full of advice on how to "git along" with Dad Eastman. Evidently, he had seen Boi in the company of the girls and was giving him a warning not to get any "durn fool ideas."

Fred was different. He didn't mind serenading the family. He claimed to be related to the wandering minstrels and was a troubadour from the Middle Ages reincarnated as a cowboy. He also said he wrote some of his own songs which he sang off key through his nose. Some of his compositions, he said, were taken from old songs to which he added some words of his own. Pete's adaptation of *Home On The Range*, for instance was:

Oh, give me a home,
Where the buffalo roam,
Where the deer and the antelope play.
Where often is heard, an encouraging word,
And moon and the stars in sky where they stay.

Sometimes his reincarnated troubadour spirit overcame him, especially at night and Dad Eastman would have to tell him to get back to the bunkhouse so everyone could get some sleep. "You'll need it in the morning." Boi wondered if Fred was merely happy-go-lucky and half-joking or if he really believed some of the line he put out.

Although Fred had not been with the Eastman ranch

very long, his gregarious nature and out-of-tune guitar got him acquainted with some of the townspeople. On Sunday mornings after the Eastmans had gone to church, he would jump on his horse and head to a certain widow's place just outside of town. Of course there were no secrets in Greenhills and word soon got around as to reason for Fred's visits. On his way back, he would stop at Mr. Horndecker's for a quick game of checkers. It was soon relayed to Mrs. Eastman what Fred was doing on Sunday mornings.

"Chester, I don't think you ought to keep Boi around that man," said Mrs. Eastman one night when the troubadour showed up late.

Mr. Eastman had thought about it himself earlier when Horndecker mentioned Fred's weekly visits to the widow. When "the minstrel" showed up one moonlit night, Mr. Eastman left his porch swing and talked to Fred about his trysts. "I've been hearing in town about your Sunday visits to the widow's house. What's going on?"

"Sure, Mr. Eastman, I go up to see Silvie. She's a fine gal, that Silvie. I think I've found me a woman as she and I seem to hit if off real good. We've been thinkin' 'bout hitchin' together. I didn't plan on tellin' nobody 'til we decided fer sure."

"What's holding you back?" asked Mr. Eastman.

"Well fer one thing, would ya still give me a job if we wuz ta git hitched?"

"Well, sure, if you could still do the job – don't know how that would work out," pondered Mr. Eastman.

"Jest think, I could have bacon n' eggs, toast, oatmeal n' coffee ever mornin' and be here as soon as I would be if'n I wuz bunkin here," said Fred with a faraway look.

"Let's see how that looks in the morning." He bid Fred goodnight and went into the house.

As the summer wore on, Fred became more amorous and frequent in his trips to the "widders." The strolling minstrel played his guitar in the long evenings and regaled the Eastmans with every cowboy song in his repertoire plus a few of his own compositions. Then one day he announced his intentions. He and Sylvie were going to the county seat and get "hitched." Since neither he nor Sylvie belonged to a church, he thought that would be best. Now, if Dad Eastman would give him the morning off — he'd be back by noon. Away they went with Dad Eastman's blessing, Fred in the saddle and Sylvie behind on Fred's black horse.

Boi was out riding the fences when he heard a horse coming up from behind and Fred yelling and whooping…"Yiipee, Cayaa!" as he whirled his lariat and let it fly encircling Boi. He would have pulled Boi out of the saddle had Boi not held tight to the saddle horn.

"I got me a woman!" he shouted coming alongside Boi. "Now, whaddya think o' thet?"

"Congratulations," said Boi. "Guess that's what you've always wanted, isn't it?"

"You bet! An' thisis fer keeps!" he shouted as he retrieved his lasso and rode off hollering and whooping!

※ ※ ※

Summer came to an end. Elaborate preparations were being made for the girls' departure for school. Clothes were carefully laid out, shoes, hats, purses and personal things, together with school material and some of the books the three older ones would need. Now they would be joined by their fourth sister.

"Oh you'll find out soon enough what you'll need after you get there," said Mary to Katy. "Don't worry about it."

"Did you say Dad has taken care of the entrance fees?" asked a nervous Katy.

"Yes. He's opened a bank account to take care of all of us. Whenever you need some money, just write a check and make sure you keep track of what it's for."

"I've never written a check," Katy's voice showed

rising apprehension.

"Don't worry," said Mary. "I'll show you. It's very simple." The questions kept coming right up to the time the train came rumbling and hissing with bell clanging into the little station at Greenhills.

The wheels squeaked to a stop and the conductor swung open the door lifted the floor plate and swung down with a foot step. Boi and and Katy stood to one side. They had not yet gone beyond the hand holding stage. Boi wondered if he should kiss Katy good-bye, there were so many hugs and kisses going around. She looked at him with a kind of expectation. Boi found himself saying, "Will you write me sometime when you are in school?"

"Of course I will, if you will write me," she answered. Boi gave her a peck on the cheek, turned red and dropped her hand just as her Dad came over to say goodbye and she turned to give Jenny, Rachael and her mother hugs and kisses.

"Board!" called the conductor and the four Eastman girls waved and shouted goodbyes to those at the station. Katy was last and, turning to look once more at the group, looked right at Boi.

At that moment, Boi felt a warm wind rush through him

and he knew it was a special farewell meant only for him!

"Where's my suitcase?" called a frantic Katy.

"They're all in here in the overhead racks. Dad put them in here," assured Mary. Dad Eastman looked down the train to make sure the trunk that all four shared had been loaded onto the express car.

"Board!" shouted the conductor again and he picked up the foot step and deftly swung himself up the steps into the open doorway of the rail coach.

The train, with its manifest of beloved passengers, moved away slowly behind an engine heaving steam and belching out great plumes of black smoke. It gained speed and grew smaller in the distance until at last it disappeared from view among the brown hills of autumn. The scene was watched silently from the station platform by five people, standing in a strange trance of sadness, apprehension and joy, knowing that the special joys of the past summer were also receding into nothing more than memories.

🕉 🕉 🕉

Boi wondered what had happened to him until he realized he was in the company of his Advocate. He wondered if that was all he was to be given to see into the reality of another life. His Advocate assured him that he could continue his life as before but that it might not be as happy as it had been in earlier times. Boi pleaded with the Advocate to let him see more.

V

Fall came with its glory of painted leaves. The maples turned crimson and the cottonwoods turned golden before they released their seeds on little parachutes of silky fibers. In the soft autumn sun, elm trees reflected their glow of pure yellow around the Eastman house and across the barnyard into the pasture beyond. Cool nights came again to herald an approaching winter.

Boi joined Pete, Fred and Mr. Eastman to round up cattle to ship to the city where they would be sold to the meat packing plants. There were some in the herd that Mr. Eastman wanted to keep for breeding to build up his herd. Boi had learned from Pete and Fred how to cut out certain of the ones he wanted to keep and corral the others to be shipped.

"Here's a letter for you," shouted Jenny as she rode up on the girls' horse.

"What does she say?" asked Jenny handing it to Boi, excited to hear what her sister would write to Boi, not thinking it might be private and personal.

Boi looked at the letter and recognized Katy's neat and

smooth handwriting. He told the Eastman's one time that you could always recognize female handwriting from the carefully formed and gracefully written letters. Mr. Eastman had laughed, thinking of his own hardly legible handwriting.

Dear Boi,

School has been exciting. My teachers are great. Would you believe I am taking math again? My other subjects are literature, history, English and music.

They also require PE (which stands for physical education!) for all freshmen, both the girls and the boys, separately, of course.

Studying keeps me busy day and night. When I am not at the library, I am doing math at home in the evening.

Mary and I have a room together. It almost seems like home except the room is smaller but of course, we don't do much of anything but study. Mary has declared a major. It is music! You remember how she was always playing on the piano at home? I think she will tune Fred's guitar when we come home.

I will write Mother and Dad, Jenny and Rachael as soon as I finish this.

I sure wish you were here. You could help me with my math. I do miss you and everyone. I will write more news to them which they can share with you.

Now I wrote first and you owe me. I will be expecting a letter from you real soon.

Yours very truly,
Katy

Boi did not tell Jenny about the underlined words but Jenny knew something was in the letter that made Boi's ears redden.

"We got letters, too," said an excited Jenny. "When you get home we'll read them to you. They have a lot of information in them about school, Mary's music and what Lucy and Vivian are doing. They have a room together in the floor below Katy and Mary."

The following Sunday Boi wrote:

Dear Katy,
Jenny brought me your letter when we were rounding up the cattle your dad was shipping to the packing plant. I sure did enjoy getting your letter. I would have written sooner but I didn't have your address. I guess your folks had it. The letter probably would have gotten to you if I had sent it to the college, I suppose they know where all the students live.

Sounds like you are having an exciting and busy time at school. I can hardly wait until I come next year. By that time I will have enough saved to make it through the first year, then after that, maybe I can find a job like Edwin and Wilfred did.

Your Dad offered to lend me enough money to start the second semester but I thought I would wait until next fall.

Nothing much has happened here—same as before you left. I sure do miss <u>you</u> and Mary, Lucy and Vivian. Your folks tell me you will be home for Thanksgiving. Oh, boy! I can hardly wait.

<u>*Very sincerely yours,*</u>
Boi

Thanksgiving came and with it the train loaded with people going to see families. It stopped at Greenhills with half of the Eastman family while the other half, plus Boi, waited on the station platform. The train slowed, wheels squeaking to a stop and the conductor opened the door, lifted the stairway platform and swung down with the little step. "Watch your step," he intoned as he had done thousands of times before.

Shrieks and squeals filled the air as Vivian, Lucy, Mary and Katy came down the steps and rushed to throw their arms around everyone, followed by excited jabbering about school and questions about what had been happening at home.

Boi was standing between Jenny and her mother so was included in the hugging and kissing that enveloped the entire family. When Katy came to Boi, she gave him an extra strong hug and kissed him full on the mouth which predictably made Boi's ears redder. He realized from the reception that he was now a full member of the family.

Thanksgiving was a festive time. The house was full of girls, running and talking. In and out. When in, talking, talking, talking. So much to tell. Boi and Mr. Eastman were often out on the range, milking cows and doing jobs around the ranch. The day of the "big bird," as Rachael called it, found a table full of sharpened appetites to match the savory fragrance that floated out of the kitchen.

In spite of all the bustle, ranch chores, and coming and going, Katy and Boi found time for conversation. Katy was full of her courses, enjoying all of them and telling Boi about them. Boi did a lot of listening. She did have some trouble with math, though, and she brought her book home hoping for his help. They sat at the dining room table in the evenings and Boi wondered if part of it was so she could sit close to him. For whatever the reason, he liked it.

Mrs. Eastman wanted to hear what Katy had learned

from her music professor. After one evening of entertainment, Mr. Eastman made the comment that it "was pretty heavy stuff."

"Not quite the forte Fred plays on his guitar," observed Boi to a round of laughter.

"Speaking of Fred, how are he and Sylvie getting along?" asked Lucy, which opened a bevy of other questions about friends and relatives.

The days went by faster than "the cattle train on its way south," noted Mr. Eastman when Sunday came around. In the morning they went to church, including Boi who had become an "almost Methodist" ("what else could I be in this environment," he wise-cracked when they teased him about it). The afternoon was filled with last-minute packing to make the 4:55 train.

Amid more hugs and kisses, this time Boi and Katy were full participants. With Boi's reddening ears, the girls climbed the train steps just as the conductor, looking at his big watch that he withdrew from his vest pocket, shouted, "BOARD!" As the train slowly started moving, the girls crowded at windows and waved. Boi saw Katy at a window blowing him a kiss. The train gathered speed and soon was disappearing down the tracks. Boi did not know this was the last time he would see Katy.

🕊 🕊 🕊

Another chill wind blew through Boi and he felt his Advocate standing beside him.

🕊 🕊 🕊

A few weeks later, the Eastmans received a letter from the college notifying them that their daughter, Katy, was in the infirmary for a short period of recuperation. It explained that it was school policy to notify parents of any illness that required more than simple medication.

In the same mail came a letter from Katy explaining that she had only gone to the health center for a cold and they decided to put her in the infirmary for a few days. She thought it was silly to go to bed with a cold, but Vivian had come to see her and told her that she had the same ailment last year and they put her in bed for three days. They were careful about an outbreak of flu since they had had an epidemic of pneumonia and lost two students, explained Vivian. Katy assured them that she would see them at Christmas.

Mrs. Eastman was very upset. She recalled three years ago when Vivian had a similar experience and the two deaths that occurred at the same time. She told Mr. Eastman she was going to see Katy — maybe bring her home if she didn't improve very soon.

She left on the very next train. "I just want to make sure Katy doesn't get any worse and do whatever I can to help get her well." After four days Katy seemed ready to return to class and her mother returned home.

Mrs. Eastman had been home a week when a second notice came informing them that Katy was back in the infirmary. "This doesn't sound good at all," Mrs. Eastman told her husband. "I'm going back there and find out what has her down and do something about it."

"Maybe I should drive up and bring her home?" pondered the rancher.

"When I get there and if I see it's serious, I'll call you to come."

One day dragged to into another. For a week there were long faces and not much to talk about. Each one echoed Rachael who spoke for all of them, when she said simply, "I sure hope Katy gets well soon." At each meal, family prayers were said. Unbeknownst to Boi and the others, prayers were being said at college by the three older sisters, as well, who had become alarmed at Katy's return to the infirmary.

Then a call came from the mother and Mr. Eastman

made arrangements with the cowhands and drove off. What he found was a daughter who was not conscious. The parents and their three daughters stood by the bed. Katy opened her eyes, then slowly closed them without a word and took her last breath. Mother, Father and three sisters were silent as the shock began to dissolve into a torrent of tears and screams.

When the news was relayed to the three at home, another flood of tears drenched the room. Boi could not contain his weeping and went out of the house and down to the tepee where he had first met the three sisters. He sat on the branch and stared back at the four sticks while tears wet his face.

Soon after he left, Jenny and Rachael came after him. He scooped them into his arms and all three let their tears and sobs melt together in Boi's strong hug.

Setting them down, Boi walked to the tepee. "I guess we should take one of these out now," as he fingered one of the poles.

"No, don't," Jenny sobbed. "We should keep it there for her memory."

"How about putting it in the middle?" said Rachael.

"That's a good idea," agreed Boi. "How about standing it straight up in the middle?"

"Good, good," said both girls at once.

Boi put the pole in the middle which made it taller than the other three. "That will mean she has returned to God."

The funeral service was held in the Methodist Church and it filled with people to overflowing. The townsfolk were attached to the Eastman family and their six girls. They knew, of course, how Boi had been taken into the family, and was working for Mr. Eastman, but none knew the attachment Boi had with Katy.

Boi's mother and father each sent comforting letters of condolence to him and to the Eastmans. Edwin made a special phone call and the two brothers talked about the pain of losing things of such great value. Knowing that he still had a firm anchorage in his own people gave him some measure of comfort. He knew they loved him as much now as they did when he was a lad, even though they were scattered now and busy establishing their own families. All of them, that is, except Frankie who was still at home and in school. He thought of Frankie and the incident at the blacksmith shop when he feared his negligence had killed his younger brother. He wondered now if that long-ago childhood incident was somehow a portent of this loss?

At the cemetery, people assembled for the burial. There

had been a rain the day before that left the sod wet and the long-bladed grass to the family plot was spongy. The Eastmans and Boi stood near the casket while the Methodist minister gave a brief eulogy. Jenny and Rachael stood close on either side of Boi. He wondered at their leaning toward him, but knew it was somehow connected to the time when they and Katy had discovered him at their tepee. There was a tree at one side of the cemetery. A blue sky bathed the site and as Boi glanced at the branches of the tree, he saw a yellow breasted black-tie meadowlark as it gave a song that reminded him of the meadowlarks he heard on his first explorations.

It was a long time before sadness didn't overwhelm the spirits of the Eastman family and Boi. The loss of Katy was felt keenly by everyone. What had been jolly times around the dining table became sober recollections of things Katy had done and said. She had been the one who always had a special knack for saying something funny and making everyone laugh. Even if what she said wasn't funny, it would inspire one of the others to expand the comment to bring gales of laughter.

Now the conversations were quiet. The sober looks on each face told feelings of the terrible loss. Boi became almost totally silent and the family knew how he felt.

When he did speak, it was usually to Jenny and when they were alone.

One day Mr. Eastman came in and talked to his wife. "I've noticed Jenny and Boi are spending time together on their horses. Do you suppose Katy's death is bringing them closer?"

"I wondered the same thing," she replied. "I saw how Boi was becoming attached to Katy and now that she's gone, he's making up for it with Jenny to console him."

"I suspect it's mutual consolation," said the rancher. "Katy and Jenny were probably the closest of the two girls."

"More than that, I've thought," said Mrs. Eastman. "I still remember how sure Jenny was that Boi was a carnie and that he was evil. She has long since found out how wrong she was, perhaps she feels penitent about it."

"I think it's more than penitence. I think their feelings toward each other is a natural rebound from Katy."

Boi and Jenny had many conversations about Katy and how they missed her. As their conversations grew, so did their reliance on each other for emotional support. With Katy gone, both felt a loneliness that each filled for the other. But the mutual feelings began to grow into a deeper fondness.

"Do you like me as much as you did Katy?" Jenny

suddenly asked during one of their conversations.

Boi was startled. He had asked himself the same question. He looked at her upturned face that was so like her sister's, yet different; her mouth that looked as though she was about to smile at some secret she held inside; her nose slightly upturned like all the Eastmans; her straight brown hair and large brown eyes that looked deep into his hidden self...

"Well?" she said at his hesitation.

"Of course I do," he blurted, "but…"

"But what?" prodded Jenny.

"Well, I was thinking about what my mother told me one time about us boys. You know there are five of us. She said to us once that she loved each one of us. We were each one different but she loved each of us for our differences."

"You loved Katy," said Jenny slowly. "Does that mean you can love me differently?"

Boi swept her into his arms and kissed her full on the lips. Then as he so often did, blushed bright red. At that, Jenny grabbed Boi and returned his kiss and a hug that expressed her affection.

"I guess we must be in love," she said.

"Of course. I have wanted to say I loved you since Katy died. When she left, something in me left with her. Now you're bringing it back."

"Does that mean you loved Katy more than you can ever love me?" pressed Jenny.

"No," replied Boi, taking Jenny in his arms for a quick hug. "In the case of us boys, my mother made it clear that her love for each of us was not a calculation of how she loved one or the other."

"So, you said when Katy died, something within you left. What was in you that left with her? What am I bringing back that she left behind?" pursued Jenny.

"I'm not sure what it was or what you have," said Boi in a deliberate voice. "I guess it's when someone leaves you, you have the feeing that you'll never see them again."

"Won't you see them in heaven?" queried Jenny.

"Of course, but…"

"But what?" Jenny thought she would pry out of Boi what seemed to be stuck in his mind.

"You mentioned heaven," said Boi brightening. "I have thought a lot about it, *everything*, your house, barn, horses, cattle, pastures, sun, moon, stars —everything including you and me and all the people on the earth, or who have lived or will live, what can God be like?" Boi had a faraway look in his eyes that Jenny didn't understand. She grabbed him around his waist, laying her face on his shoulder.

"I don't understand what that means," she said.

"It means that if you and I and everyone else are only a speck of the infinite creation we must be a part of God, and a part of God would make us part of creation. If creation has no beginning or end, then we must be in it now. We are in it now, as well as being alive…"

"I don't understand what you're saying – it's almost like a foreign language. Where did you learn all that?" asked Jenny.

"I don't know for sure, I guess. Maybe from some of the science and history books at school." Boi rubbed his chin and continued, "I guess it came mostly from my parents; they talked to me about these things even when I was a kid. But when I'm out riding alone, especially at night and I look up and see the stars, I think about stuff like this. I write to my dad, too, and tell him what I'm thinking and he writes back; we have philosophical discussions by mail." Boi admitted this with a surge of gratitude for what his parents had taught him.

"Did you ever talk to my Dad about this?" Jenny asked.

"Oh, yes. We've had some real good conversations. He said he's had similar thoughts about it all."

The romance between Jenny and Boi flourished. By the time they were almost finished with college they were making plans to get married. Boi had graduated and Jenny was a year away from finishing, they were anxious to get married and start their lives together.

"Jenny, you should finish school," both her parents agreed. "Tell you what," said Mr. Eastman. "You finish school while Boi and I build you a house."

Though they had talked about going back to the ranch, Boi wasn't sure it would be a good thing. He had taken a few courses in drafting and construction and had thought about going into business somewhere in a city. Fate intervened.

They decided to build not far from the old Eastman home place. Boi and Mr. Eastman had completed the framing and were closing it in, when Mr. Eastman suffered a heart attack and was sent to the hospital. Jenny had been coming home on weekends but this time she didn't return to school and stayed home to help while her mother was at the hospital looking after Mr. Eastman.

By this time, both Vivian and Lucy were married with small children, and Mary was engaged. The Eastman household was now reduced to Boi, Jenny and Rachael who also came home from college on weekends. When Mr. Eastman had recovered enough to go home, all of the girls came to see how well he was recuperating and to fuss over him.

While Mr. Eastman was getting back on his feet, Boi helped with the cattle and continued work on the little house. Jenny helped with much of the finish work. When her sisters saw her in painters overalls and cap, splashed with spots of paint, they knew it wouldn't be long until she and Boi would be married and living in their own home. They joked about whether Jenny or Mary would be first to the altar.

Finally, the house was finished and furnished. The two cowhands stayed on and this relieved Boi of much of the responsibility for looking after the cattle. With Boi less occupied and the house completed, he and Jenny set a date for the wedding.

It was a beautiful day. All of the sisters came to help with the preparations. They filled the church with rows of beautiful yellow daisies, lilacs, and honeysuckle that filled the church with a soft perfume. Years before, they had thought a wedding would be for Katy and Boi, but Katy was now only a memory, as soft as the sweet fragrance of the flowers.

Jenny was aware of the tradition of her sisters to wear their mother's wedding dress. All six of the girls had grown only two inches taller than their mother but all had the same body measurements she had when she was married to their dad.

"But should I wear the wedding gown that Katy would have worn? I feel I'm taking her place. I'm not myself," she wailed to her mother.

"Would you like to have a different one?" her mother asked.

Jenny's eyes blinked as they began to fill with tears. "No," she said slowly, "only, well…" she sobbed softly into her mothers arms.

Jenny and Boi talked about who would officiate at the wedding. "I think your father should take part," said Jenny. "Yeah. I was thinking about that," replied Boi.

Boi's family came to the wedding, along with his father. Before the ceremony Wilfred and Edwin took him aside and engaged him in light-hearted banter, purporting to give him the real "low-down" on what he was committing himself to. Being veterans of marital bliss, they had several serious, mostly redundant pieces of brotherly advice for him, as well. Frankie, who was now a lanky fifteen-year-old (Boi scarcely recognized him), stood more-or-less on the perimeter of the commotion as an uneasy, but nonetheless fascinated spectator. Boi's mother and sister were dressed more fashionably than he had ever seen them and were wearing the corsages he had given them. His mother told him how delighted and reassured she was with his choice of mate and that she was convinced he was destined for a beautiful life, especially so when accompanied by such a charming girl. This made Boi swell with pride. He knew that he was bringing someone into his family who would be loved as much as he.

It was after the ceremony that Boi said they were truly married with *two* clergy performing it. Jenny laughed and said that it meant they were truly man and wife, till death did them part. "Even after death I don't think we'll part," said Boi.

"Maybe you're right, maybe death is only a beginning and that we don't really vanish into nothing," said Jenny.

"It's hard to believe that we may already be into eternity but just don't realize it," said Boi with a faraway look. The two sat in the porch swing, arms around each other talking about their lives ahead. They knew it would be a beautiful life, just as his mother had promised.

The newlyweds moved into their new home and happily finished some forgotten places and things they had overlooked. As they settled in, they were especially pleased when family and friends came to visit. When one of Mr. Eastman's cowhands left, Boi found he was needed to help with the cattle business.

Not long after Jenny and Boi set up housekeeping,

Rachael and Mary both married. The five surviving girls were now married and starting families. Joy and good times filled the growing Eastman households. Mr. Eastman's health, however, was failing and he was finally stricken with a fatal attack.

Again, grief struck the family as they placed his body besides his parents and Katy in the family plot. Rachael had married a young man who was a rancher so now that Mrs. Eastman was alone, Boi and Jenny moved with their children into the home place and gave their little house to Rachael and her husband. They thought of it as a family legacy.

They hadn't been in the family home more than two years when one day Boi said to Jenny when they were alone, "Since your dad died, your mother doesn't have the life in her that she used to have."

"I've noticed that, too," replied Jenny sadly. "She used to say when we were all at home that when Chester dies, she will die with him. Then we all laughed when Katy piped up, 'What if one of *us* goes first, maybe me, then what's your schedule?' We had fun over that at the time, but now we're faced with something none of us expected."

And Mrs. Eastman did join her husband within a few years. The entire family, now consisting of five in-law men and eight grandchildren, stood at the burial site of Mrs. Eastman who was laid to rest next to her cherished husband, Chester, and beloved daughter, Katy, who died too young.

Life went on. Boi and Jenny had two more children who, together with the older two, were an indescribable joy to them. By now, Boi was deep in the cattle business with Rachael's husband. One late evening when the children were put to bed, Boi was sitting in the big chair in which his late father-in-law once sat. It was close to the piano where Jenny was playing some bit of classical music. She had learned to play nearly as well as Katy.

Suddenly she stopped and turned to Boi. He had his eyes shut and Jenny could see his face was wet. She squeezed into the chair next to him brushing away his tears said, "You still miss Katy, don't you?"

"Yes, of course, but then I miss your dad and mother and it's hard to believe, I miss their parents, as well as the generations before them and my own family and the generations before them. Think of all the people in the world, Jenny, who were born, lived their own special lives and then died."

"Even as we will," added Jenny.

"I often wonder why the Creator would make it so...

and not only people but animals, birds, even snakes…"

"Ohhh," moaned Jenny jestingly. "Rattlesnakes!"

"Yes, every living thing including trees, grass, bushes, lightning and thunder — everything on this earth that ever was or ever will be and even the world itself. Astronomers say that even the sun and stars have lives — very long lives to be sure but they exist by the same pattern of birth, life, and death. It's strange, isn't it, that we're all in it together?"

Boi could tell that Jenny was dozing off. He picked her up and carried her to bed. When he talked philosophically, she would always go to sleep.

The days flew by and picked up the weeks to bid years go with them. Their children went with the years and Boi and Jenny hardly kept up with them.

"Mother, school starts and I need some books, paper and pencils; mother I need a new dress, and some shoes and socks; Dad, what college should I go for. The one you and mother attended doesn't have the curriculum I want; Mother…Dad…" and on it went.

The household was a happy one. "Like the one I grew up in," said Jenny to Boi, "You remember that, don't you?"

"Of course. I even remember thinking that when I grew up and had a family, I hoped it would be as happy."

Jenny smiled.

"What are you smiling at?" asked Boi.

"Oh, I was thinking about the time you were invited to dinner on Sunday and you tried to help Dad chase old Bossie when she got out of the pasture."

"What got me was how Katy called to her and tickled her ear and she went back where she got out," Boi chucked.

Time did go with the days, weeks, and years. They were measured out by family celebrations of Thanksgiving feasts and jolly times at Christmas and birthday parties. The events were made more happy by visits from sisters and their families who took nostalgic delight in being in the old home place once more. They especially looked forward to visits from Boi's family, all of whom had a great fondness for the pastoral setting of their place.

The children were growing and one by one they went off to college. "It gives me a strange feeling to see the children growing," said Jenny one day. "They're doing like we did only in their own way."

"Nothing stays the same. Everything changes." replied Boi. "Look at Greenhills. Smitty's station is gone, Horndecker closed his shop years ago, the train doesn't pick up passengers any more, the realtor left, the little theater is closed, and look at the number of boarded up windows on Main Street. Greenhills is beginning to look like a ghost town. We're lucky to have a grocery store left."

Changes were everywhere. Both boys graduated from the university and went to Kansas City to make their careers. Both girls also finished college. Boi and Jenny would have been alone except for Rachael and her family with whom they spent much time.

Misfortune can come to good people in the same way good fortune blesses bad. Boi had seen that often enough to tell Jenny that he thought the Creator must be neutral in the affairs of men. Jenny was reminded of that when she learned that Boi was killed by a drunk driver as he was walking across the street to the post office. Jenny was stunned. Children and sisters all came to share in her grief.

🕊 🕊 🕊

At the cemetery, Boi stood with his Advocate. Boi was silent. So, too, his Advocate for a long time.

"Do you recognize your own place in the Eastman site?"

"Did I die?" Boi hesitatingly asked.

"It depends upon what you mean by dying," replied the Advocate. "If you mean by having passed mortality, yes. You are returning to immortality where you were before."

"Are there many mortal lives I can experience?"

"Yes. You may have as many as you like. It would be more accurate to say, you may repeat mortality as often as you want, but you will notice you have less desire this time than most."

"Others? What others?" asked Boi incredulously.

"You don't remember your previous one, do you?"

Boi hesitated. "I recall the life just passed. The family I grew up with, a sister and fours brothers that my father was a small-town preacher, and my mother was a very lovely and patient woman. Then I found the Eastman family in Greenhills, and Katy who died young and Jenny…OH! Jenny, where is Jenny?" Boi suddenly remembered.

"Look for yourself," the Advocate answered.

Boi looked about at what he could see. Slowly an image began to form, like a photograph developing in a tray of chemicals. "I'm not quite able to see…" he told his Advocate. "Oh, Jenny! Jenny," and he felt a rush of emotion as her face came into sharp detail. He moved to where he could embrace her. A gentle breeze rustled her dark hair, which had strands of silver throughout to show that time for her, too, had passed.

Boi thought she must surely see him but she gave no sign of recognition. Then he discerned the truth. She was looking through and beyond him, *in the same way Katy had at the train station when she went off to school.* When he turned to see where her sight was fixed, he saw others standing around. He was at a ceremony of burial.

"Whose casket is being lowered into the ground?" he asked Jenny, but he couldn't hear an answer, nor could he hear the words of the minister who was reading something from his little black book.

Turning again towards Jenny, he saw the familiar dark brown eyes flushed with tears. To his astonishment, two tall young men stood beside her…THEIR SONS! and two young ladies…THEIR DAUGHTERS! and…and…four sisters or was it *five*? He looked again and there was KATY! She turned to him and smiled!

Turning back to his Advocate, Boi asked what all this was about? He saw Jenny and their children but they didn't see him. Then Katy was with the other five sisters and she smiled at him!

"Do you recall when I asked if you wish to go on and you said yes? I gave you a second chance and now you see Katy. Look around you and you will see others who came to your memorial."

All about him, Boi could see his family, the Eastmans, friends, children from years ago. "Is this a sleight of hand trick?" he asked the Advocate.

"In one sense it is, since it appears at only one particular time of mortality. But there is no time to immortality. Time is merely a way by which mortal existence is measured."

"You mentioned my *other* life. Was what I remember about Jenny and Katy and all the others, was that another life?"

"Think back. Do your recall being married to anyone else, having a different family…a different boyhood?"

Boi was silent. What could the Advocate possibly mean? There was most certainly no other one than Jenny and he most certainly has had only one family in which he grew up and only one family that he had taken as his own.

"No, I don't recall any other life."

Boi detected wry humor in his Advocate's next words. "No you don't. Of course you don't. Memory is a quality of the mortal state, and once you have left mortality, memory ceases. The fact that you can still recall means you have not quite left the mortal state. Once you have, you'll not recall any part of your former existence. I simply was not sure you had left the present. You made a good choice when you did not give up when Katy died."

Boi looked back again toward Jenny who was being led away by their children. She stopped and turned her face full on Boi. The glance was dazzling bright and she was smiling.

She waved a handkerchief that had the sweet perfume of lilac and honeysuckle floating on kisses she sent to him.

Through a gathering mist and by the last light of his fading mortal vision, he saw something else. Down alongside the clear-flowing waters of Rock Creek where a tepee had once stood, something was slipping silently through the tangled overgrowth of tall grass and trees.